BROKEN WINDOWS,
BROKEN LIVES

BROKEN WINDOWS, BROKEN LIVES

Adrian Plass

HODDER AND STOUGHTON
LONDON SYDNEY AUCKLAND TORONTO

British Library Cataloguing in Publication Data

Plass, Adrian
Broken windows, broken lives
I. Title
823'.914[F]

ISBN 0 340 50265 7

Chapter One

"My name's Dennis. I'm a maladjusted boy."

The voice was small and anxious. By the time I turned round the speaker had vanished, presumably behind a rather majestic fir tree standing a few yards from the door marked *Visitors* where I stood trying to summon up enough courage to ring the bell. Ever since starting the long walk up the pleasant tree-lined drive leading to the school buildings, I had been nervously aware of a small, awkward figure, dodging from tree to tree as it shadowed my slow progress towards the scene of the dreaded interview. Now it had spoken to me. It was called Dennis. It was a boy. And it was maladjusted. Presumably, I reflected, Dennis was one of the children I would be caring for if my application for the post of Housefather was successful. I was a little surprised. Surely they weren't supposed to know that they were maladjusted, were they?

I decided that, as Dennis had spoken to me, I ought to speak to him. After all, for all I knew, my prospective employer was studying this encounter with great interest from some nearby window. It was my very first meeting with a 'disturbed' child. I tried to sound warm and therapeutic as I addressed the fir tree.

"Errr . . . Dennis, I'd love you to come and have a little talk with me. If you want to, that is."

For a little while nothing happened. Spring sunshine rippled through the clear downland air. A telephone rang somewhere in the school buildings. With a bit of luck my prospective

1

employer would have to leave his window to answer it. I was about to speak again when Dennis popped his head out from behind the tree like an inquisitive squirrel, then popped it back again, apparently overcome by the thought of the awful risks he might be incurring through this courageous act. I cleared my throat.

"Do you errr . . . live here, Dennis, or errr. . . ?"

Obviously drawn by the sheer sparkle of my conversation, Dennis slid tentatively around the wide trunk and stood with his back jammed against the tree, eyes wide with a curious mixture of panic and wistful longing. Suddenly shocked, I realised that I had seen that look before, in the eyes of an Irish Setter, rescued by a friend from someone who had beaten his beautiful pet viciously, and totally without cause, throughout the first year of its life. There had been that identical cringing fear, battling with the same yearning promise "You just give me the smallest, tiniest reason and watch how I'll wag my tail and be happy."

But this was a boy, not a dog. How could Dennis have got into this state? I shivered slightly.

"It's nice to meet you, Dennis. My name. . ."

The clanging of a distant handbell interrupted my latest conversational ploy. Dennis was instantly diverted by this new and more immediate cause for panic. He quivered with urgency.

"School!" he piped, breathlessly. "Gotta go ter school!"

To my surprise, he turned his body and flung his arms as far round the tree as they would go, pressing one side of his face against the rough bark, as though bidding an affectionate farewell to a close friend. I watched, fascinated, as he gave the trunk a final, fond pat, then turned and hurried towards a brick building on the other side of the car park. His journey took rather longer than it might have done owing to the fact that his limbs seemed to operate quite independently of each other. This made for a rather odd mode of progression. One arm, for instance, would fling itself out to the right, dragging the rest of him wildly in that direction, but almost immediately the opposite leg might make a determinedly violent lunge to the left, without any reference to anything else, the overall effect being that of a pair of arms and legs attempting to escape from a body. Somewhere in the centre of all this activity, the essential Dennis travelled in an average direction, rather than in a straight line. As I gazed at this strange sight I was struck by the remarkable similarity between Dennis, with his wispy figure, large ears and nervous disposition, and one of my favourite fictional characters, A.A. Milne's Piglet. It occurred to me that there must be many Heffalumps in little Dennis' life. I wondered how old he was. Eight, perhaps?

By now, Dennis had arrived at a short flight of stone steps leading up to a large open doorway at the end of what I supposed must be the classroom block. He paused on the bottom step, each limb coming to rest in its own time, and looked back in my direction. Cupping a hand round his mouth, he shouted something in a high, excited voice. It sounded like, "We're having public vice in school today!" but I wasn't sure.

Public vice? Surely no school would teach public vice as a subject, and, as for Dennis, I couldn't imagine him finding the nerve to indulge in any vice, let alone a public one. Puzzling. Very puzzling!

The idea of working with children was something quite new for me. All my life I had wanted to be an actor, a film actor to be precise. My dreams of big screen stardom were very persistent. They survived a shambolic school career, and led finally to a real place, on a real course, at a real acting school. Here, the reality of what I soon discovered to be a very tough and demanding profession, trampled heavily over my fantasies, and I was forced to think again about my future. I left the acting course half-way through, hot with the shame and disappointment of failure, but still managing a quite spurious air of cool, masterful detachment. Most adults seemed to be fooled by it. Those who weren't, I carefully avoided. But what was I going to do? Whatever the career I chose, it had to offer at least a faint echo of the significance and power that I had enjoyed in my thespian dreams. Where was a twenty-one year old with few qualifications, a frail self-image and not much self-discipline to find such a situation? It was a fair measure of my naivety that, when a friend drew my attention to an advert at the back of a social-work journal offering the post of Housefather to an enthusiastic, but not necessarily experienced person, in a boarding school for maladjusted boys, I decided that I had found what I was looking for. Other than having been a slightly strange boy myself, I knew nothing about boys; nor did the term 'maladjusted' convey anything at first, beyond a vague impression of some sort of physical incapacity or oddness. After one or two enquiries I discovered that it actually referred to children who were not physically disabled but, for one reason or another, couldn't cope with normal school and family life, although all those I asked, including experts, seemed unable to be precise in their definitions. Most of these children, I was told, came from broken homes, or difficult family situations of various kinds. Boarding schools like Stapley Manor were intended to provide the kind of expert care and education that might give these unfortunates some hope for the future.

Armed with this very basic information, I sat down in the corner of my local, the King's Head, one evening, spread the advert out on a little wooden-topped, wrought-iron table in front of me, and resolved that I would leave the pub only when I had made a firm decision about applying for the job. I could have discussed the matter with my girlfriend, Annie, but I knew that she would have been adult and sensible about it. I wanted to dream my way into a decision before telling her what I was going to do.

I wasn't a heavy drinker usually, but that evening I seemed to float on a sea of beer as my mind played with increasingly sentimental images of tragic but beautiful children who, in large filmic close-ups, wept with gratitude as they understood that I, a cross between Danny Kaye and Doctor Barnardo, was able to offer them all the love and strong support that had not been theirs in the past. By the time I had downed my fourth pint, this moving picture was beginning to bring tears to my eyes. I felt a burning need to communicate my excitement about the institutional Pied Piper role that awaited me in my wonderful new job. The trivial processes of application and interview were forgotten. Those children needed me. They were going to have me! Standing up, I made my way unsteadily to the bar where the meltingly attractive, red-haired landlady, Kate, smiled as charmingly as ever as I placed my glass down with exaggerated care on the gleaming bar top. I took a deep, serious breath, and fixed her with my eye.

'Kate,'' I said, in Shakespearian tones.

"Yes, dear,'' said Kate, leaning her elbows on the bar and resting her chin in her hands. She had a wonderful gift of being able to look at you as if you were far and away the most important thing in her life.

"Kate!'' I repeated, my voice slightly choked with emotion. Kate radiated empathy. "*Yes*, dear.''

"It's not fair, Kate. It's jus' not fair!''.

"No, dear,'' said Kate. "You're right. It's *not*.''

"I mean. . . they never had a—what's it, did they?''

"They *never* did,'' agreed Kate, "never!''.

"So th' thing is, Kate. Th' thing is. . . that some-one—someone, right?''

"Someone, dear, yes.''

"Someone's gotta help 'em!'' I flung my arms out in dramatic emphasis, accidently catching my glass and sending it skimming away along the polished surface of the bar. Kate caught it with a practised hand and, with barely a blink, resumed her attentive position.

"Someone *has* got to help them, dear. You're absolutely right.'' Her blue eyes were swimming with sympathy.

"So,'' I said, shifting my position slightly as something rumbled uncomfortably in my stomach, "the point is Kate - should I. . . or shouldn't I?''

"What do *you* think, dear?'' People study for years to learn what Kate seems always to have known.

I stood up very straight, swaying slightly as I pondered the question. Again in my mind's eye I saw the touching scene in which thanks were lavished on me by slavishly adoring kids, their large brown eyes brimming with tears of new-found happiness. I brought my fist down with a thump beside my glass.

"I'll do it! That's it! I've decided! I'll do it!''

"You *will* do it, dear,'' Kate's smile was warmly encouraging.

I nodded my head slowly, an unfocussed little smirk of satisfaction on my face, and made my way towards the door, almost overbalancing as I paused to pick up my job advert on the way. At the door I looked back. Kate gave me a little wave and another encouraging beam. I was momentarily overcome by sugary feelings of gratitude.

"Kate," I called, as I opened the door.

"Yes, dear."

"Kate—I jus' wanta say thanks for—for understanding. Thanks!"

"It was *nothing*, dear," said Kate, as I went out of the door and closed it quietly behind me.

By morning, most of the extravagant emotion of the night before had been replaced by the unfamiliar symptoms of a mild hangover, but my decision remained intact. After all, whatever else the job might be, it couldn't be very difficult. All it called for was a willingness to show kindness and concern to a group of children who were all too ready to receive it. What could be easier? I sat down at the little table by the window in my bedsit, high up overlooking the Pantiles, and carefully composed a letter of application in which I tried to give the impression that my departure from acting school was the result of a moral conversion from selfish ambition to profound awareness of the needs of others. I blush when I remember that letter. But it seemed to do the trick. Within a few days I received a letter signed "A.E. Rowley, Headmaster", asking me to attend for interview in a fortnight's time. I was elated. Any sort of success had the effect of recharging the batteries of my self-esteem at that time. I hurried round to Annie's flat and told her the good news, hoping that, having by-passed the discussion stage with her, she might just say "Jolly good" and leave it at that. She was pleased, but I sensed a note of reserve in her enthusiasm. I heard myself babbling foolishly.

"It's not all that far, Annie. You'll be able to come down on the bus at weekends and meet the children, and I can come up here on my days off to see you." As an afterthought I added, "If I get the job, of course, that is!" I chuckled as though the idea of my not getting the job was just a mildly amusing joke.

Annie put a mug of coffee in front of me, then knelt facing me, smoothing out her long honey-coloured hair with one hand. "It's not that."

Annie could be disturbingly wise about me at times, though she usually allowed me to hang on to a few harmless illusions about myself. I really didn't want her to say anything that would spoil the way I felt about the sparkling new career that I was envisaging.

"What is it then?"

"It's just. . . oh, it's nothing! I'm just being silly. I'm sorry, I shouldn't have said anything."

I ground my teeth. She was doing it again. Starting to say something I didn't want to hear, then stopping and apologising before she actually got round to saying it! I shifted my weight to the edge of the chair and breathed in heavily through my nose.

"Annie! Will you please just tell me what you thought. I want to know."

Annie took a sip from her coffee and studied my face doubtfully. "Are you sure? You won't get angry?"

I replied in the manner of one who has been reasoning unsuccessfully with a half-wit for hours. "Annie, if you've got something helpful to say, then of course I want to hear it." My careless laugh emerged as a slightly manic cackle. "Why should I get angry, for goodness sake?"

We both knew that Annie was going to say it in the end, and we both knew that I was going to get angry. The preceding dialogue was a well-established routine. I leaned back in my chair, lit a cigarette and did my best to look calm and objective.

"Carry on. Just say what you think, and we'll discuss it, and . . . well—discuss it."

Annie took her life in her hands. "It's just that I wonder if you're going to be. . . well, tough enough inside for that kind of job." She glanced up at my face much as the inhabitants of Pompeii must have glanced up at the first ominous puffs of smoke from their volcano.

Narrowing my eyes, I blew a long thin stream of smoke, and spoke with barely restrained exasperation. "Yes, yes! Go on. I don't understand why you've stopped. I haven't said anything, have I?"

Annie went on bravely. "I mean, you're not really even very good at taking criticism, are you?" She screwed her whole face up, flinching in advance.

For a moment I was speechless, shaking my head slowly from side to side, mouth open wide in shocked amazement.

7

"Annie, how can you say that? Honestly—you tell me you've got something useful to say, and, naturally, I'm only too pleased to listen to it, and then you. . . you say something stupid like that! I'm sorry, but I just don't understand you sometimes! Don't you want me to do well?"

Annie was looking at the floor, her face hidden beneath a tent of hair. When she spoke I could tell that she was on the verge of tears.

"I never said it would be useful, just. . . "

"I mean, if what you're saying is that I don't appreciate destructive criticism, then I agree with you. But you know as well as I do that if someone's got something constructive to say, then I'll listen, and probably act on it. Sometimes I don't think you understand me at all!"

The tired old 'I appreciate constructive criticism' argument had stood me in good stead for years. Actually, I hated any criticism, constructive or otherwise; Annie was quite right. That was what was making me so angry; nor was I sure, even now, exactly what point she was making. Suddenly I was filled with the cold despair that always flooded through me when someone or something reflected weakness or unpleasantness in me. Not that this or any other emotion was capable of shutting me up for long.

"Here we go!" I spoke with weary monotony. "Now you'll cry, and I'll feel guilty, and you'll say it was all your fault, and that'll make me even more angry because I know it's my fault really, then you'll cry again, and I'll feel guilty again and then you'll lose your temper again, and I'll sulk for two hours!"

There were times when I loved Annie so much that I surprised myself with the pureness of my reaction to her. At the conclusion of my gloomy list of predictions, she sat back on her heels, pushed her hair away from her face, and after a brief attempt at remaining serious, broke into a giggle.

"Well, now that we've done all those awful things, let's go and have a drink, shall we?"

Exit cold despair, but I still needed her blessing. When we reached the bare hall at the bottom of the stairs I stopped and, putting my hands on her shoulders, spoke with rare humility.

"Annie, do you think I'd be alright in that job?"

Sensing that it was a real question, she gave me a very straight look from large grey eyes, and answered quietly but definitely:

"I think you could get very good at it, but some of those children won't be all that much younger than you are, and they're not going to go out of their way to make you feel alright when you feel as if you're failing. That's all I meant upstairs really. Anyway," she steered me firmly towards the door, "I'm here, so we can always talk about—well—things, can't we? If you want to, that is."

As we crossed the square towards the little knot of drinkers enjoying the brittle April sunshine outside the pub, I had no doubt at all about the answer to that question. There would be rows, conflict, childishness on my part, but, yes, I would certainly want to.

The day of my interview began with one of those spring mornings that are jubilant in their freshness and tender warmth. By the time my bus—one of the more ancient members of the Southdown fleet—crossed the county border into Sussex, my mood was one of mellow contentment. The world was full of new things, in a new season. It seemed a good omen. Perhaps my season had come.

Actually arriving in Stapley was a bit of a shock. As the bus rumbled away down the narrow High Street, leaving me standing in my only suit at the bus-stop outside *Tingley, Grocer*, I felt a sudden sharp stab of anxiety about the formal encounter that was due to happen in approximately one hour. Up to now the whole thing had existed only in my head and on a small piece of printed paper. Now, as I looked around at the very clean, olde-worlde cottages of Stapley, guarded on three sides by the massive, sensual swell of the South Downs, I wished that I was back in a place I knew well, surrounded by people I knew well, people like Annie. I gulped slightly at the thought of Annie. If I did get this job, then I would probably have to live here, in Stapley. How often would I see her? How sure could I be that, with me tucked away down here, she wouldn't find someone who needed much less mothering and careful diplomacy than I did, someone who wouldn't make her cry with his childish behaviour and shout her down when she talked sense. A wave of numbing insecurity broke over me as I stood in this horrible little village, on this horrible spring morning, thinking about this horrible job that I probably wouldn't be able to do anyway. Why should I care what happened to children who couldn't 'adjust', whatever that meant? It was probably mostly their own fault, in any case. Look at me. My own parents had split up when I was young, and things had been very painful—very difficult. I was alright, wasn't I?

I trailed miserably along the picturesque main street, vaguely registering a small art gallery, the obligatory dusty, secondhand book shop, a smattering of cream-tea cafes, a pub or two, all the things that visitors demand from the average, unspoiled English village. Usually I would have enjoyed exploring at that peculiar station-platform pace that one reserves for things like local potteries. Today, only the pubs had any attraction for me, and I had already passed two of them. I toyed with the idea of simply not turning up for the interview. There was a bus back to Tunbridge Wells in less than an hour. I could just get on it, and that would be that. I pictured the meeting with Annie later when she'd finished work at the hospital. She would be bright and excited. Wanting to know every detail.

"How did it go, David? What was it like? Tell me what they said!"

When I tried to picture her face as I told her that I hadn't even got to the interview, a shutter slammed on my imagination. She would be furious—scathing. I knew Annie. Supporting me was one thing, letting me get away with being that weak was quite another. I decided that I would go into the next pub I came to, and make a final decision over a pint of lager. I could see, in the distance, what looked like a pub sign, extending welcomingly out over the pavement. My progress was arrested a few yards further on, however, by a much smaller, wooden sign pointing down a narrow alley between two thatched cottages. It said simply, TO THE CHURCH.

The whole business of 'God' was just one of the guilt areas that formed an unruly and perpetual queue at the gateway of my attention. Four years previously I had been confirmed at Saint Bartholomew's Church in Tunbridge Wells, and for a short time afterwards I had rushed around in a frenzy of evangelical activity, hoping that my heavy expenditure of energy would be paralleled by an equal increase in virtue. When I discovered that it didn't work out in that sort of automatic way, I collapsed in a moral heap, exhausted, and since that time had never regained my early enthusiasm. I still thought of God, though, as being in some quite indefinable way, a person who had claims on me. I had postponed the sorting out of these feelings, largely, I think, because I was so annoyed with Him for not co-operating with my personal plans for spiritual development.

"Anyway," I had complained to Him one day, "you don't even exist."

Stapley Parish Church, Saint Peter's, turned out to be a small but attractive building with a low, broad-based spire. It stood at the far side of a pleasant green area below and behind the High Street shops and houses. Further on still, a river wound slowly through the valley between lush, grassy banks. Around the side of the church, a footpath led towards the river, crossed via a wooden pedestrian bridge, and disappeared temptingly into a clump of trees at the foot of the hills. I stood for a moment on the edge of the green, invaded, despite myself, by the sheer peace of the scene, and wishing that I could run like a little boy, along the path and over the river to find a hiding place somewhere among the trees. I had never felt less grown up.

When I tried the door of the church I found, to my surprise, that it was unlocked. So many weren't. Pulling the massive old oak door open, I stepped inside and stood transfixed for a moment by the sight that met my eyes. The church was full of daffodils. On every ledge and in every corner, the yellow trumpets blew a fanfare of colour. The effect of all this natural neon against the ancient grey of the stone walls was more than beautiful. It was awesome. There was no stained glass in the simple little building, just a series of tall, narrow, slightly tinted windows. Through one of these, the sunlight poured generously over the dark Victorian pews, turning the dust on the old stained wood into tiny shining specks and adding a glow of pure gold to the streams and pools of yellow blossom.

I felt as if I'd been ambushed.

"Did you do this?"

My quite involuntary and rather loud question to God embarrassed me terribly. I turned quickly, fearing that someone might have heard this loony talking to himself just before they opened the door, but there was no-one. I walked slowly up the centre aisle and knelt on the long leather cushion beneath the communion rail. As I gazed at the very simple silver cross that hung above and behind the altar, part of my mind told me to stop over-dramatising myself and go. Another part asked God a further question.

"Should I go and have this interview?"

No voices from heaven. No writing on the wall. Just, when I stood up and turned round, the daffodils, the sunlight, the old walls, containing in some way the essence of newness and growth. There was a 'Yes' in the air.

As I left the church and strode back across the green towards the High Street, I glanced at my watch. Still plenty of time to get to the school if the directions I'd been given were accurate. Down to where the houses ended and the road curved away to the right, and look for a little turning on the left called Backbreak Hill. It wasn't difficult to see how the hill got its name. For a quarter of a mile or more I laboured upwards between fields of grazing cattle, until the lane flattened out for about a hundred yards before curling round the base of an oddly regular, cone-shaped hill. I could see, set back from the road, a clump of buildings of various sizes that I supposed must be Stapley Manor. I was already sweating from the steep climb I had just done. Now, as I reached the bottom of the drive and read the words *Stapley Manor School* on a large notice-board beside the gate, I started to perspire again with apprehension.

My little encounter with Dennis was actually rather reassuring. It was only as I watched him disappear through the door of the school block after calling out his cryptic message, that I realised how much I had been worrying about having to cope with big aggressive kids who wouldn't be interested in my control problems. Annie had been quite right. Well, perhaps they would all be like Dennis. If so, then I really didn't have much to worry about, did I?

I turned, took a deep breath, and pressed the bell-push beside the *Visitors* sign.

Chapter Two

"Mr. Harper, what would you do if you came into a room and found two boys engaged in a vicious fight, with all the others standing around in a circle cheering them on?"

"Ah!" I said, significantly, as though I had been eagerly awaiting just such a question. "Well, now let me see . . ."

"Would you break it up straight away?"

Something in the voice of the pear-shaped little matron warned me that, as far as she was concerned, I would be ill-advised to plump for breaking it up straight away.

"Well, no . . . not straight away, but. . ."

"You mean you'd just let 'em kick each other to death, do you?" the deputy headmaster, Mr. Ashton, a grizzled, practical looking man, leaned back in his chair and looked at me as if I was a blocked drain. Something told me that this was far from being the first occasion on which the matron and the deputy had crossed swords over this particular issue. Which of them should I ingratiate myself with? Or should I be an impressively independent thinker?

"No, of course I wouldn't let them kick each other to death." I sniggered politely in recognition of the deliberate absurdity. "No, what I would actually do. . . "

"Wouldn't a lot of it depend on which boys were involved and what would be best for them as individuals?" The matron, nodding encouragingly, almost slipped off the edge of her chair in her earnest desire to convert me to her way of thinking. It was a straw. I grasped it.

"Well, of course," I said, "yes, of course it would depend on. . . on that."

A snort from the other end of the table drove me into a hasty qualification.

"But, having done that I would, without any question, err . . ."

"Bang their heads together?"

"Err. . . yes—no. . . perhaps."

I could feel a light sweat breaking out on my forehead. If these two experts didn't agree, how on earth was I supposed to know the answer? It was with considerable relief that I realised the central and most important member of the panel, A.E. Rowley, was leaning forward to speak. I hoped he'd change the subject.

"Let us hypothesise an alternative crisis," said the headmaster impressively. He half rose in his chair and adopted a dramatic posture. "There is a boy. He is a large aggressive boy. He is clutching an object in one hand. As he approaches you it becomes clear that he is no longer in control of his actions. He loudly declares his intention of castrating you using the rusty razor blade with which he now wildly saws the air. You are weaponless. What," demanded A.E. Rowley, "would you do?"

I knew I had turned white. Did such things happen in these places? Surely Dennis. . . The headmaster was still poised dramatically, waiting for my answer. I sighed inwardly. Job or no job, I couldn't be anything but truthful about my reaction to the horrific scenario that had just been outlined. The matron might have used psychology on this hypothetical maniac and the deputy might have grappled heroically with him, but I knew what I'd do, and it was no use pretending otherwise.

"I would run away as fast as I could."

Mr. Rowley sank slowly back into his chair, a lopsided smile illuminating his face.

"So would I," he said. "That was just a sanity test. Don't worry—you passed."

Their differences temporarily forgotten, my three interrogators fell about laughing, leaving me to wonder yet again what kind of strange little world I had entered since ringing the doorbell two and a half hours ago.

The door had been opened by a neatly dressed, middle-aged lady with kind eyes, who introduced herself as Mrs. Philips, the school secretary.

"You must be Mr. Harper," she said, smiling warmly as she sensed my nervousness. "I'm so glad you found us alright. We are a bit tucked away, aren't we, but it's a lovely spot. Can I get you some coffee? Mr. Rowley has arranged for one of the boys to give you a guided tour of the school before anything else happens. That'll be in about five minutes."

I gratefully accepted the offer of coffee and followed Mrs. Philips into a small sitting-room, already occupied by one other man, suited neatly like myself, but unperspiring and horribly confident looking.

"Mr. Harper—Mr. Glander. You'll be up against each other this afternoon."

Glander winked smoothly at me and raised his hand about three inches from the arm of his chair in a perfunctory gesture of greeting. As the secretary disappeared, presumably to get my coffee, I took stock of my rival. He was older than me and much more powerful physically. I was tall and thin. He was below average height, but thick with muscle. Beneath short-cropped dark hair, the eyes were lazily arrogant. He could kick the truth into any shape he wanted. He was the kind of man who had always made me feel weedy and ineffectual. As Mrs. Philips reappeared with my coffee, I wondered what she thought of him. She smiled at him in exactly the same way as she smiled at me. Why? I suddenly wanted to be with Annie very much, hearing her say that she didn't fancy bull-necked masculine types who couldn't care. . .

"Can I get you anything else, gentlemen?"

I very much wanted to use a toilet, but I feared that in my present state of diminished self-worth, my request would emerge in a high, piping little voice, thus confirming what I imagined to be Glander's opinion of me as a gormless, negligible twit. The child in me wanted to take this nice kind lady's hand, and trot along beside her to find the lavatory. Instead, I shook my head with as much nonchalance as I could muster and stirred my coffee slowly, hoping that Glander would not notice how my hand was shaking slightly. As Mrs. Philips went out, closing the door behind her, I took the coffee spoon out of the cup and in a fever of confusion, popped it suavely into the top pocket of my jacket. I retrieved it almost immediately, glancing up with burning cheeks to see if Glander had noticed. He had, of course.

"Where you been before?" He spoke with a strong Midlands accent. The faint note of ridicule in his voice was infuriating.

"Before what? Sorry, I don't know what you mean."

"Before this," said Glander. "What sort of places have you worked in before—with kids I mean?"

"Oh, I see what. . . yes. Actually I haven't worked with children—I mean kids—very much. In fact, not at all really. Not really. . . at all. Not actually worked with them as such."

My pathetic attempt to imply an extensive experience of voluntary work with children was cast aside.

"You haven't got a chance, friend. I've been dealing with kids for ten years. I've worked on my own with more than fifty of the little sods at a time. You wouldn't know where to start, would you?"

It did cross my mind to ask him why, with ten years behind him, he was applying for a job that, even I knew, was at the very bottom of the career ladder, but I lacked the spirit. He was quite right. I wouldn't know where to start. I didn't have a chance. The sooner this farce was over, I thought gloomily, the better.

"For instance . . ."

Apparently animated by the thought of his own expertise and experience, Glander turned in his chair to face me, resting his elbows on his knees and leaning forward to wag his finger in my face.

"Do you know how to really hurt a kid without leaving a single mark on his flesh?"

Glander's trousers were horribly tight around his thighs.

"No," I said quietly, "I don't want to know . . ."

"Well," said Glander, as though I had pressed him eagerly for the information, "you do it by cracking 'em really hard with the edge of a wet towel—must be wet mind. Dry leaves a mark. That's where most people go wrong. Got to be wet."

I was saved any further instruction in the art of bloodless brutality by the entrance of Mrs. Philips, accompanied by a boy who, at first glance, seemed not unlike a junior version of Glander except that his hair was a bush of flaming red.

"Right, Mr. Glander," said the secretary briskly, "if you'd like to go with Colin, he'll give you a first class tour of the whole place, and bring you back here in about half an hour." She spoke brightly to the boy, who must have been fifteen or sixteen.

"You'll answer all Mr. Glander's questions, won't you, Colin dear?"

The boy glared venomously at Glander and grunted something that sounded like "With luck I will" but I wasn't sure. Glander rose from his chair, hitched his trousers up unnecessarily and followed his young guide through the door, walking with that peculiar bandy-legged swagger that seems to be obligatory for people like him.

"Won't be long, Mr. Harper", smiled Mrs. Philips. "Your turn very soon."

Left to myself again, I realised as I finished my coffee that my heart was hammering away wildly. The unfamiliarity of my surroundings, Glander's grotesque confidence, and a rather ominous quality surrounding the red-haired boy, all combined to make me feel profoundly uneasy about whatever experiences the rest of the day might hold for me. I wasn't going to get the job anyway, so why hang about and invite trouble? If I were to slip out quietly. . .

"Sorry to keep you waiting, Mr. Harper. Alright to go now? Here's your pilot, ready and willing."

Mrs. Philips stepped aside to reveal my young guide for the next half hour. I rather hoped it might be Dennis. It wasn't. It was an older, much more normal looking boy than Dennis. He had a pleasant, somewhat mournful face, with large dark liquid eyes that seemed to me full of sensitivity and intelligence.

"This is our Tom," said the secretary fondly. "You'll look after Mr. Harper won't you, Tom?"

"Yes, Mrs. Philips," said Tom pleasantly, "I'll do my best." I was struck by how well spoken he was.

Seconds later we were outside, standing beside Dennis's fir tree at the top of the drive. Tom, who didn't seem to me in the slightest maladjusted, asked very politely what I would be interested in seeing first. That was easy.

"I think, Tom," I replied tensely, "that, first of all, I would be interested in seeing the toilets."

As my tour of the campus proceeded I became increasingly mystified by my young companion. His manner was a little funereal, but he seemed so balanced and nice, that it was difficult

17

to believe he was anything but normal. First of all he showed me the little individual gardens, most of which, I learned, were worked by boys who were hoping to pass a CSE exam in Rural Studies eventually.

"Do you have a garden, Tom?" I asked.

"No," said Tom, shaking his head seriously, "that's not my thing."

Moving on to the far corner of the grounds I saw the big roomy cages where guinea pigs and rabbits were kept as pets by some of the children, and from there we passed along a narrow path between high hedges to the football field, lying immediately at the base of the cone shaped hill which overlooked Stapley Manor.

"That's what we call the Peak," said Tom, pointing across the grassy expanse. "Quite a lot of people go up there to play games and things. There's a boy called Dennis who goes up there just to roll down again."

I shaded my eyes and peered up at the hill.

"It's a long way to roll," I said. "Doesn't it make him sick?"

"Always," said Tom mournfully, "very sick."

I had already established that Tom did not own any of the small animals and that he very much disliked football. I wondered if games on the Peak might be more to his liking. I asked him.

"Games on the Peak," said Tom gravely, "are not my thing. But," he added with an odd note in his voice, "I have been up there."

We moved back towards the buildings, Tom dutifully pointing out the gardener's shed, the camp store, the headmaster's house, the school block, and the tennis court at the front of the building from which the village of Stapley could be seen nestling attractively in the valley below us. I looked at the uneven grass court then glanced up enquiringly at my guide. He shook his head sadly. I nodded comprehendingly.

"Not your thing, eh, Tom? Never mind. Can we see inside the part where you actually live?"

He led the way up a flight of shallow brick steps and through a very ornate pair of French windows into a large wooden floored room containing a three-quarter size snooker table, a dartboard, a very old-fashioned radiogram and an assortment of boxed board games on a green baize table in the corner.

"Games room," said Tom.

"Ah," I replied, "so this would be the place where you play err . . ."

"Games," supplied Tom kindly. "Lots of people play games here in the evenings and at weekends."

"Not you?"

He just shook his head. Perhaps, I thought, we are beginning to really communicate.

Tom explained that there were two living units or 'Houses'. One, the original Stapley Manor, was known simply as the 'Old House', the other, a modern brick building attached to the end was, unsurprisingly, referred to as the 'New House'. Each house was able to accommodate fifteen boys and was made up of a dining room, a games room, a television room and bedrooms of various sizes. Tom lived in the New House, although he would much prefer to have been in the Old House, he said, and as he never watched television and wasn't particularly interested in food, there wasn't much to do indoors.

"You do sleep do you, Tom?" I asked flippantly.

"Yes I do," he said, without a flicker of a smile. He looked at me for a moment. "Would you like to see my bed?"

I followed the slim, slightly bowed figure into the comparatively uninteresting surroundings of the New House and up some stairs into a long corridor with bedrooms on either side. Tom stopped at the third door down on the right and pointed to one of the four beds, each with its attendant wardrobe and bedside locker, that took up most of the space in the room. Tom's bedspace was amazingly tidy. Small personal possessions were arranged with intricate care on the locker top and clothes were neatly folded and put away in the wardrobe drawers which he opened and displayed with quiet pride. Hesitantly, he indicated a photograph stuck to the side of the locker nearest to the bed. It was a man and a woman posing with two young children. One of them might have been Tom. I looked up.

"How long have you been here, Tom?"

"Four and a bit years," said Tom. "We'd better go."

Down a different flight of stairs we went, along another corridor, and out through some kind of boot room into the sunny yard that separated the living quarters from the school block. I looked at my watch.

"Five minutes left, Tom. Anything else you think I ought to see?"

Tom began his customary doleful headshake, but stopped suddenly as an idea struck him. A new light appeared in his eyes. Was it possible, I wondered, that I was to discover what Tom's 'thing' was?

"Would you like to see my favourite place?" he enquired tentatively. "The place where I feel most at home?"

I felt warmed and flattered. Fancy this boy taking me into his confidence after such a short acquaintance. Perhaps I had relationship-building qualities that had never had the chance to emerge before.

"Of course, Tom," I said. "Lead on."

He set off at a surprising pace, heading for a line of poplars that bordered the piece of cultivated ground at the end of the Old House. On the other side of the windbreak the ground fell away sharply, then levelled out into a small fenced area, mostly occupied by two flat round constructions with long metal poles running from centre to circumference.

Tom was standing on a low brick wall overlooking these contraptions. As I joined him on his narrow perch, he sniffed the air like someone taking a constitutional at the seaside, and threw his arms wide.

"This is it!" he cried, with a display of emotion I wouldn't have thought possible. "This is where I really belong!"

Thoroughly puzzled now, I tried a sniff myself, and felt my face screwing up in disgust. There was a horrible smell, and it seemed to be coming from directly under my feet. Looking down I realised why. At the base of the wall, two or three feet below the surface of the ground, two open sewer pipes were visible to the eye, and more than perceptible to the nose, as they transported the whole of Stapley Manor School's effluent to the disposal system that lay before us.

"You really feel at home here?"

"Oh, yes," breathed Tom ecstatically. "This is me! This is where I fit!"

As we hurried back to the school office a couple of minutes later, I felt an odd mixture of bewilderment and elation. Bewilderment because I couldn't for the life of me even begin to understand why anyone should find happiness and security

20

only in the proximity of sewage, and elation because it seemed that, despite my inexperience and naivety, I had penetrated the defences of this strange boy, and discovered a secret that was almost certainly not known to anyone else. I couldn't wait to tell Annie. She would be so impressed, even if I didn't get the job. As Tom deposited me outside Mrs. Philips' office and murmured a polite farewell, I suddenly felt that I really wanted this job. But what hope was there against someone like Glander?

Mrs. Philips seemed genuinely pleased to see me again.

"How did you get on with Tom?" she asked.

"Oh, very well indeed," I said. "Actually, there was something that. . ."

"That's marvellous!" she looked at her watch. "Now, the headmaster has asked me to take you over to the classroom block so that you and Mr. Glander can take a little stroll with him before the actual interviews begin. Okay?"

I nodded, rabbit-like in the face of her brisk and smiling efficiency.

Mr. Rowley and Glander were waiting on the steps of the classroom block as we walked across from the office. Glander was laughing about something, head thrown back, hands in his trouser pockets. Probably laughing about me, I thought. Probably telling the headmaster what a useless idiot he thought I was. Probably. . .

"Mr. Rowley, this is Mr. Harper. He's just been shown round by Tom. I'll leave him with you, shall I?"

Mrs. Philips started to walk away, then stopped and, turning back, fixed the headmaster with a stern eye.

"The interviews begin at three o'clock sharp, Headmaster. You will be there, won't you?"

A.E. Rowley, a tall, very impressive looking man in his fifties with a little tuft of 'mad-professor' hair on either side of his head, stared indignantly over his glasses at the secretary, apparently deeply hurt by the implication that he could be anything but punctual.

"Of course, Doreen! Naturally! Of course!"

As Mrs. Philips began to move away again, Mr. Rowley clapped a hand to his head and took a step towards her, as if some fresh thought had caused a minor panic in him.

"Oh, Doreen. . .!"

The neat figure stopped and turned once more.

"Yes, Headmaster?"

"What time did you say the interviews are to occur? Four o'clock was it, or. . . ?"

Mrs. Philips sighed. "Three o'clock, Headmaster. They are at *three* o'clock."

Mr. Rowley nodded wisely. "Ah, yes, of course, yes, thank you. Three o'clock, of course."

As Mrs. Philips hurried away the headmaster turned to me with an expression of real interest on his face.

"So Tom showed you round, Mr. Harper. I should be most interested to hear your impressions of the boy, most interested."

Pride swelled within me. This was my moment! As we started walking slowly round towards the back of the school block, I sought for suitable words to describe my breakthrough with this boy who had trusted me with his secrets.

"Well, actually Mr. Rowley, it was an extraordinary . . ."

"Nothing interesting about my bugger!"

Glander's voice clubbed my speech to death.

"I beg your pardon, Mr. Glander," said Mr. Rowley, switching his attention to the other man. "Did you say there was nothing interesting about your bugger?"

"That Colin! Hardly said anything all the way round and most of what he did say was effing and blinding under his breath. Kids like that—they never change. He'll be in prison before he's eighteen. Give you fifty to one on it. I've seen it all before. I've worked with a thousand Colins."

"And failed with them all? How very discouraging that must be for you, Mr. Glander."

Was the headmaster's tone deceptively mild? Glander was temporarily rendered speechless.

"Of course, we only have one Colin here," went on Mr. Rowley, "and I must say we're really rather fond of him. But," he conceded, "he is rather horrible at times—but then so am I, so . . ."

"Is smoking allowed here, Mr. Rowley?"

A little knot of boys, presumably released for afternoon break, had overtaken us as we strolled slowly towards the gardens. They whispered and pointed and laughed as they passed.

I had noticed that one was holding a cigarette packet and a box of matches.

"Smoking?" said Mr. Rowley in deeply shocked tones. "Smoking among the boys is expressly forbidden by County Council rules and is consequently not allowed in this school. Absolutely not!"

"But one of those boys was holding some cigarettes when he went past just now. I saw them in his hand!"

The headmaster gazed distractedly into the distance. "I saw no cigarettes," he said, apparently losing interest in the subject.

The boys in question had all disappeared behind a large bush about twenty yards from the woodwork shop, which was housed in an extra wing attached to the back end of the school block. It was impossible to be unaware of the fact that smoke was rising up from behind the bush in little puffs and trickles. Either the bush was on fire, or those boys were smoking.

"The little buggers are smoking behind that bush!" said Glander, revived by the sight of something punishable.

Mr. Rowley scratched his bald patch and gazed around with a perplexed expression on his face.

"Bush?" he said. "What bush?"

"That bloody bush!" spluttered Glander, pointing at the large and very substantial shrub which was still smoking gently a few yards away from us.

"You must see our bonfire . . ."

I only just caught the headmaster's words as his tall figure set off at a near run in the general direction of the sewage plant. Instead of continuing towards the poplars however, he turned abruptly to his right and disappeared down a narrow passage between two big creosoted sheds. I could hear Glander puffing and swearing behind me as I hurried through the narrow space and emerged to find myself in a small scrubby area enclosed on two sides by a thick beech hedge and concealed from the main buildings by the two large outhouses I had just passed between. In the centre of this space stood two metal incinerators, beside what looked like a perpetual bonfire, at present just a low pyramid of grey ash with a curl of smoke drifting up lazily from the centre. A boy was kneeling on the ground beside the fire, doing something to a large cardboard box with a pair of scissors. A.E. Rowley stood beside him, arms folded, watching.

"I rather suspected we might find young Robert here," he said happily. "He's making a house out of a cardboard box, aren't you, Robert?"

The boy looked up and nodded. Two things struck me. His spectacles, black-rimmed and powerful, only just managed to retain their identity. They were held together by an extraordinary collection of sticking plaster, bits of string, soldering wire and sellotape. Behind thick lenses, the eyes were crafty, fearful, excited. The other thing was the exceptionally high colour in his cheeks. A bright red spot burned on each cheekbone, contrasting vividly with the cold whiteness of the rest of his flesh. He was indescribably dirty and untidy.

"Say hello to these two gentlemen, Robert," said Mr Rowley, "and tell them what you're doing."

"'Lo!" grunted Robert gracelessly.

He picked up his cardboard box and placed it open end down on top of the rubbish in one of the incinerators. I peered at the box. He had cut spaces in its side to represent windows and a door. Eyes gleaming with excitement, he took a book of matches from his pocket and lit the paper in the incinerator under the cardboard. As the paper caught and flames started to lick up into the box and flicker through the windows, Robert spoke with profound relish.

"It's an 'ouse, see, an' I've set fire to it. An' there's lots of people stuck in there, an' they're all bur-r-r-nin' to death!"

He squatted down, staring into the flames, lost in the excitement of his fantasy, the fire's reflection dancing and leaping in the glass of his disreputable spectacles.

The headmaster looked at his watch, then he looked appealingly at me.

"Mr. Harper," he said, "I wonder if you can possibly recall whether Mrs. Philips specified three o'clock or four o'clock as the time at which the interviews are due to commence? I'm afraid . . ."

"Three o'clock," supplied Glander flatly, "and it's five-past now."

As we made our way briskly back towards the office, I remembered Tom.

"I was going to say, Mr. Rowley, about Tom, that something really rather . . ."

"Ah, there you are at last, headmaster. It's nearly ten-past three. . ."

Mrs. Philips had come to meet us.

In one sense I was quite looking forward to the formal interview. Not that I believed for one moment I would be offered the job. My brief encounters with only one or two boys had shown me clearly that I would be completely out of my depth when it came to actually helping them with their problems. But there was something about A.E. Rowley that really appealed to me and I hoped that some of the mysteries I had encountered during the afternoon might be solved during the next couple of hours.

Glander was called into the headmaster's office first, leaving me to flick nervously through an ancient women's magazine which had been left on the coffee table in the sitting room. The next forty-five minutes felt like several hours. My limbs grew increasingly twitchy and uncoordinated, and I could feel the hair on my temples becoming dank and dishevelled with sweat as I mentally rehearsed, again and again, the ways in which I might answer the awkward questions that were bound to arise during my interview.

At last Glander reappeared, looking slightly less self-assured, but rather more aggressive. He whistled viciously through his teeth as he collected his bits and pieces from the chair opposite mine. I sensed that he wanted to get away quickly without having to talk to me.

"How did it go?" I asked innocently.

He stopped on his way to the door, and shrugged as though unconcerned.

"If they want someone who can control kids, they'll offer me the job. If not, it's their funeral."

He shook his head scornfully.

"I'll tell you what. If this Rowley bloke can't even see kids breaking rules right under his nose, I'm not sure I'd want to work for him anyway. Plenty more jobs around."

He wasn't really speaking to me. He was addressing the weak blancmange-like world that I represented. As he disappeared from sight, hitching his trousers up as he went, I knew instinctively that, small as my chances of getting the job were, it was extremely unlikely that a man like Mr. Rowley would want to employ a man like Glander. For the first time a tiny seed of hope took root in me.

25

The first half of my interview, however, felt fairly disastrous. Mrs. Crompton, the matron, put a number of hypothetical situations to me, none of which seemed to bear any relation to any experience I had ever had. Granted, she also provided very strong clues to the kind of subtle, psychological responses she obviously hoped to hear about from me, but I was hampered from supplying these by constant interjections and comments from George Ashton, the deputy headmaster, who clearly favoured the practical, no-nonsense approach to problem solving. In the course of juggling my answers between these two, I became increasingly aware that Mr. Rowley seemed to be taking no interest whatsoever in what was going on. As far as I could see, the whole of his attention was focussed on one of those little square plastic puzzles where you have to get all the letters into alphabetical order. Apart from brief introductions when I came in, the headmaster's 'sanity test' was his first real contribution to the proceedings. By some miracle I seemed to have got that one right, and after guffawing loudly for a few moments, he laid aside his puzzle, peered curiously at me over his glasses, and smiled that same lopsided smile.

"Mr. Harper," he said pleasantly, "it seems quite plain to me that you know nothing about working with disturbed children - nothing whatsoever."

My heart sank.

"This is, of course," he went on, "a distinct advantage in the post for which you are applying. We shall be able to teach you how to make mistakes our way."

I started to titter, but stopped abruptly as I realised that he hadn't been making a joke.

"However," continued Mr. Rowley, "it may be that you are a little err. . . confused about some of the work that we do here. So if you have questions about anything at all, I - that is to say we—shall be most happy to answer them."

At last! My turn to ask questions.

"Yes," I said, "there are one or two things . . ."

Chapter Three

"Public *vice*, Mr. Harper?"

The headmaster's noble brow was a mass of wrinkles as he tried to make sense of what I'd just said.

"You say that young Dennis was expecting to receive instruction in public vice? How very curious."

"Well, I thought that was what he said, but I might have misheard. I'm not sure. . ."

George Ashton looked even more as though he'd like to take a dyno-rod to me. The matron was sitting up very straight in her chair with an expression of stern reproach on her face. I half expected her to reach over and smack my hand for telling fibs. She spoke.

"We concentrate on mental, physical and moral health here, Mr. Harper. There is absolutely no question of any instruction or encouragement in things that would be harmful to the children."

"I never thought. . ."

"Thought we'd got old Den on the CSE shoplifting course, did you?" queried the deputy headmaster dryly.

I shifted uneasily on my seat. This was dreadful! Why couldn't I have kept my mouth shut?

"I'm sorry—I never meant. . ."

"Oh!" The little matron's hands flew to her face as a cry of realisation escaped her. "Oh, Mr. Harper! Public vice! Oh dear me! Oh. . ."

She dissolved into helpless giggles.

"My dear Mrs. Crompton," pleaded Mr. Rowley. "Please shed light on this little mystery. We are completely in the dark."

The matron controlled herself eventually, dabbing her eyes with a pale pink handkerchief as she explained.

"I'm sorry, Mr. Harper. I can quite see now how the misunderstanding came about. You see, we found that we had a little problem—a health problem—among the older boys this morning. It looks as if little Dennis got hold of the wrong end of the stick when I announced at morning assembly that there was to be a special inspection after lunch today. He obviously thought that I said one of the boys was suffering from 'public vice', whereas actually. . ."

Her next words were lost in another choking fit of giggles.

"Whereas. . .?" A half smile was frozen on Mr. Rowley's face as he awaited the revelation.

Mrs. Crompton's handkerchief was just a sodden little pink scrap by now. Clearing her throat, and shaking her head once or twice, she continued.

"Whereas, actually, he was suffering from *pubic lice!*"

All three members of the interviewing panel exploded with laughter. The headmaster picked up his little plastic puzzle, threw it into the air and batted it across the room with the flat of his hand. In between shouts of laughter he repeated the words "Public vice—pubic lice!" with immense satisfaction. George Ashton, his face screwed up in mock disbelief, was shaking his head rapidly from side to side and banging the table in front of him with his fist, his gravelly laughter combining discordantly with Mr. Rowley's full-bodied guffaws. The matron left the room with tears running down her cheeks, only to reappear a few seconds later with a long length of pink toilet paper into which she blew her nose loudly and repeatedly.

I didn't laugh. I couldn't have laughed if I'd tried. I was absolutely appalled! PUBIC LICE? What kind of horror was this? And why were these three people able to laugh so freely about it? I, who had always liked to imagine myself a free spirit, untrammelled by petty pruderies, had never, ever talked about pubic anythings, let alone lice! I knew the blood had rushed to my cheeks. I was crimson with embarrassment and apprehension. If I were to be offered this job, would I be expected to inspect. . . surely not! A grotesque image was forming in my mind as I waited for the panel to regain control of themselves. It was a boy. A sort of composite of Mr. Rowley's hypothetical maniac, and all the other children I had met or heard about since walking through the gates of Stapley Manor. I could see him clearly now, a red-haired, homicidal, lice-ridden pyromaniac, who spent his life hugging trees and ecstatically inhaling sewage fumes. How much were they paying for this job?

"Please excuse us, Mr. Harper. We do rather relish little Dennis's verbal inexactitudes."

The headmaster was in command of himself once more. He shuffled the papers in front of him rather unconvincingly, stifled a final guffaw, and looked up at me with a puzzled expression as though he was having difficulty remembering who I was and what I was doing there. Little gusts and giggles of mirth were still erupting spasmodically from his colleagues on either side.

"Now, Mr. Harper, where were we. . . ? Ah, yes, of course. Questions! Please continue with your questions."

Mrs. Crompton and the deputy leaned forward expectantly, hoping presumably that I would come up with yet another rib-tickling query. Perhaps, I thought, they might take me on as a sort of resident source of light relief if all else failed. I took a deep breath and launched into the only area that offered any possibility of impressing the three people facing me.

"About Tom. . . the boy who showed me round. There was something—or rather he said something that I thought was, well. . . important."

There was no doubt that I had their attention now. The matron, pubic lice forgotten, was on the edge of her chair again, kindly blue eyes wide with interest, her hands neatly laid on her knees. George Ashton looked as if he'd found something rather interesting blocking the drain, and Mr. Rowley, most disconcertingly, had risen to his feet and was gazing fixedly at me, with his hands clasped firmly on top of his head.

"Tom is our oldest resident, Mr. Harper. We are all very. . . very concerned for him. I should take it as a personal favour if you would be good enough to describe your encounter with him in detail, and of course your impressions of the boy. Sometimes outsiders can. . . well, do tell us please."

For the first time since the interview began, I relaxed a little. They really seemed to want to know what I thought about Tom. In painstaking detail I described my recent tour of the school, secretly relishing the approaching climax of my tale, and the thought of the oohs! and ahs! that it might provoke in my audience. They listened without interruption, flatteringly attentive to my every word. As I finished, dry-mouthed but fluttering inwardly with excitement, I noticed with surprise that Mrs. Crompton was wiping a tear from her eye. It wasn't a tear of laughter this time, but I couldn't think what had caused it - nothing that I'd said, surely?

"Remarkable, Mr. Harper—quite remarkable!"

The headmaster sank slowly back into his chair, that strangely illuminating smile transforming his face again.

"You are the first, Mr. Harper, the very first!"

It was a gratifying response, but why was the matron so deeply moved?

"You mean the—first to know about the sewage plant and. . . all that?"

"Good heavens, no!"

Mr. Rowley thrust his head forward under his hands like a surprised tortoise.

"No, Mr. Harper, Tom has been entertaining psychiatrists, psychologists, social workers and assorted visitors with trips of that kind ever since he joined us. He once persuaded the Chairman of the Council, a rotund person, to accompany him, by way of an exceedingly ancient ladder, to the flat roof of the schoolroom block. It was only there, Tom claimed, that he felt truly comfortable."

He smiled at the confusion that must have been evident on my face.

"Tom is a very bright boy, Mr. Harper, very bright. But he has found it necessary—essential really—to postpone the more traditional achievements until certain other problems are - resolved. The manipulation of adults is one of the ways in which he, shall we say, fills in time until then."

George Ashton scratched his nose.

"It's his hobby," he growled. "It's what he does."

So that was Tom's 'thing'. I could never have guessed it in a million years! So what had Mr. Rowley meant when he said that I was the first? Something to my credit? Please God, let it be some little thing to my credit.

'When Mr. Rowley said you were the very first, Mr. Harper, I think he was talking about something else that you said."

Mrs. Crompton was no longer crying but her voice was soft and serious as she went on to explain.

"You said that Tom took you up to his room and showed you a photograph. Can you remember who was in the picture?"

I thought for a moment.

"As far as I can remember, there was a man and a woman and two young children. I sort of assumed one of them must be Tom. It was just a guess though. . ."

"You were quite right, Mr. Harper. One of the children was Tom, the other was Tom's younger brother Justin—JD they call him, short for Justin David. That picture was taken about ten years ago when Tom was five and Justin was four. It's the only picture left that's got Tom and his mother in the same photograph."

I sensed some sort of tragedy.

"But why is there only one. . .?"

"Tom's mum tore the rest up. That one escaped somehow. You see, when JD was born, Mrs. Verne suddenly developed a quite irrational dislike for little Tom. She hated herself for it - she's a very nice lady actually—but nothing seemed to change the way she felt."

I swallowed hard. If I could have left without fuss at that moment I would have done. I had a feeling that Tom's story was going to dig into secret, tender places inside me. The matron's eyes watched mine as she continued.

"She managed to cover it up for quite a long time—she did very well, she really did—but. . . well, children sense things. As Tom got older he began to realise that JD was getting something from his mum that he wasn't. Not toys or food or anything like that. Mrs. Verne was scrupulously fair about material things - that was the easy bit. What Tom was missing out on was real, genuine affection from his mother. We're not really sure what happened then, but it seems that Tom spent most of his time trying to earn—to buy back—his mum's affection. And of course the more he tried to do that, the more angry and guilty his mother became, until the way she felt about Tom was right out in the open and she began to treat him very badly indeed."

"You mean. . ."

"She would hit him, say sarcastic things to him—that sort of thing. And Tom. . . well, he still didn't understand what was going on, so he'd try even more desperately to make her love him."

Mrs. Crompton's eyes were unnaturally bright.

"It must have been. . . awful. Anyway, one of the things she did to hurt him was to tear up all the photographs that they were both in. She did that just before he came to us, when he was about ten. He had to come anyway, you see. It was affecting everything—school, friendships, the other members of the family - everything. He goes home at holidays, but only for short periods, and she's never visited him once in all the time he's been here. His dad comes now and then. A nice man, but weak. So you see. . . that picture is very important to Tom. . ."

"And the point is," interrupted George Ashton, "that in all the time he's been here, we've never got him to talk about his mother once. It's all been 'strictly private—keep out', that sort of stuff. I've tried—twice. Once, he ran straight away from me, down the drive, out the gate, up to the top of the Peak, and we didn't see him for three hours. The other time, he screwed his eyes shut, put his hands over his ears and sat in the boot room like a little wise monkey for a whole morning. He knows we know he knows an' all that. I think he even quite likes us, but. . ."

Mr. Rowley leaned forward and spoke very directly to me:

"For Tom to voluntarily invite you, even by a single gesture, to look at that photograph on his locker, is a major step forward in that young man's life. There are no miracles in the work we do, Mr. Harper, but every now and then there are moments, significant and sometimes heartwarming moments. This was just such a moment, and we thank you for it."

Soon after that the interview was over. There were many questions I had not managed to ask but I was feeling shell-shocked by the whole experience and I was quite content to ask for information on purely practical matters during the last ten minutes. The headmaster confirmed that if my application was successful, I would be expected to live in a small single flat in the Old House. My duties, he said, would be concerned with the day-to-day running of the house and the general welfare of the boys. I would wake them in the morning, supervise them in the evening and put them to bed at night. I nodded confidently at this, despite the fact that I had not the faintest conception of how I would approach or perform these tasks. George Ashton added that I would be expected to carry out running repairs on locker doors, tables, windows, and anything else that needed attention in the house. This was rather alarming.

I had never met anyone less practical than myself. I seemed to need an armful of tools just to change a plug. I didn't reveal my incompetence - after all, perhaps I could learn as I went along.

As I flopped down in an armchair back in the little sitting room, I closed my eyes wearily and wondered what I would do if Mr. Rowley offered me the job before I left this afternoon. Could I really cope with boys like Dennis and Colin and Robert and Tom—poor old Tom. Come to think of it, Tom wouldn't be in my house. He'd be in the New House, but that didn't mean I wouldn't see him because. . .

"Mr. Harper. Wake up, Mr. Harper!"

It was Mrs. Philips. I struggled to my feet, bleary-eyed and heavy with the beginnings of sleep. I couldn't seem to get one side of my body level with the other. I felt a wreck.

"It's alright, Mrs. Philips. I wasn't really asleep—just. . . just resting."

"Of course, Mr. Harper. You deserve a rest. It's been a long afternoon for you. It's just that Mr. Rowley wondered if you would care to join him for a nice cup of tea and a piece of cake or a biscuit before you leave."

She smiled meaningfully at me.

"I really think you should, Mr. Harper."

"Err. . . yes, yes of course. I'd like to, Mrs. Philips. Thank you—I was just wondering though, is there any chance of being able to use a phone before—before that?"

Understanding and warmth positively flowed from the secretary.

"Why don't you come and use the phone in my office, Mr. Harper? You can be nice and private in there. No one will disturb you."

Two minutes later I was alone in the tiny office. The telephone, a friendly shape, sat on the desk in front of me. Through the net-curtained window I could see Dennis' fir tree (that was one of the things I hadn't asked about), and beyond it, sharp and distinct against the blue expanse of the sky, the very top of the hill that they called the Peak, the place that Tom had escaped to when someone tried to coax his personal demon from the back of his troubled mind to the front. I knew a little of how Tom must have felt that day. There were things in my own past that, even now, I was careful never to remember. Was there a risk of stirring those things up if I spent all my working life with these

33

chaotic, troubled children? Probably. Almost certainly. Could I handle that?

I dialled Annie's number.

"David?" said her voice a few moments later. "Where are you? How did it go? Did you get it? What's. . . ?"

I broke in.

"Annie, I've got a feeling Mr. Rowley's going to offer me the job—in a minute, I mean. But I'm not sure. . ."

"Not sure? Not sure about what? David, what aren't you sure about? Tell me, David!"

I could feel how much Annie wanted to be right beside me, talking sense, reassuring—all the things she was so good at.

"Annie, I'll have to live here. I'll hardly see you—we'll hardly see each other! You'll get fed up with. . . with. . ."

"What are you worried about, David?"

Annie's voice was suddenly very calm and even.

"I just told you. . ."

"What is it really, David? Please tell me."

I hadn't got time to tell Annie off for taking a short cut through yet another of our familiar argument patterns.

"Annie, the children here are—some of them are very - unlocking."

"Unlocking?'

There was silence on the other end of the line as she pondered the word that had sprung quite unbidden to my lips.

"Unlocking of you, you mean?"

'Well—yes, in a way. . ."

"David."

"Yes, Annie?"

"You need unlocking. The only question is whether this is the best way to do it. It wouldn't be fair to use the children as a sort of therapy. I don't mean that. On the other hand, there are things you'd understand that lots of other people wouldn't."

She paused.

"Darling, I think you'll find it difficult for a while, but. . . well, maybe you're ready to have a go at something difficult. It's up to you in the end though. I'll be happy whatever you decide. Oh, and David. . ."

"Yes?"

"I love you."

"I love you too, Annie. I'd better go—see you later. In the King's Head?"

"Oh. . . yes, okay. See you later, darling. I'm sure you'll make the right decision. Goodbye."

Mrs. Philips led me along a brick path that curled between widely spaced silver birch trees set in a wide area of soft green grass between the office block and the road. The headmaster's house turned out to be a big red-brick building with a curiously irregular shed-like construction attached to one side. The secretary pushed the front door of the house open without knocking and ushered me along the hall into a pleasant sitting room where Mr. Rowley and one other person were sitting at a low table laden with all the usual paraphernalia of teatime. The other person was a boy. He seemed vaguely familiar, but I couldn't for the moment remember where I had met him. The headmaster looked up at me over the top of his glasses.

"Mr. Harper! Good of you to come—you met Robert earlier, did you not?"

Robert? The boy at the bonfire? Could this scrubbed, tidy boy with perfectly preserved spectacles possibly be the same disreputable urchin whom I had witnessed earlier burning imaginary people to death in a cardboard box house?

"Say hello to Mr. Harper, Robert."

"Lo!" grunted the boy through a mouthful of cake.

It was Robert.

"Robert came over to ask my opinion on his readiness for a parental visit," explained Mr. Rowley.

"No I didn't! I come over t'see if I's smart enough fer my dad!"

Robert's voice sounded gruff and uncompromising, but there was something in his eyes as he barked at the headmaster that must have come very close to being fondness—or even love.

Mrs. Philips spoke from behind me.

"The last time you saw Robert he was probably looking rather different, Mr. Harper. But when his father comes to visit, he likes to be nice and smart, don't you Robert?"

"'Ave to!" snorted Robert, "else 'e goes off agen!"

He jerked a thumb disrespectfully at Mr. Rowley.

"'E lets me get dirty 'ere. 'E says its orlright to be like I am, 'e does! Dunno why," he added, rather spoiling the effect.

A telephone rang out in the hall. Mr. Rowley and Mrs. Philips excused themselves, leaving me with Robert who was smacking his lips and eyeing with relish the rest of the large chocolate cake on a glass stand beside him. I panicked suddenly. Supposing Robert tried to help himself to more cake. Should I say anything? Should I stop him? Was I in charge of him at the moment, or. . . oh, heavens! His hand was reaching out to take a piece . . .

"Err. . . Robert, I don't think you ought to take anything until you've asked Mr. Rowley, do you?"

Robert withdrew his hand and glared coldly at me.

"Wassit got to do with you? 'Snot your piggin' cake!"

My mouth had gone dry. I knew that my voice shook slightly.

"I could be coming to work here," I said, hoping to impress Robert with the fact that I might soon have official responsibility for him.

"'Ope not!"

I could hear Mr. Rowley's voice indistinctly in the hall as he spoke on the telephone. Why didn't he come back and rescue me? My dignity was being threatened by this unformed, graceless boy. If he did try to take more cake, should I physically restrain him, should I ignore him, or should I take the cake away from him? I wished I was a million miles away. Suppose the headmaster came back in to find Robert and I struggling on the floor with bits of cake flying around everywhere. What would he think of me? To my intense relief Robert seemed to have abandoned the cake idea, but he was doing something else. His hand was in his mouth. He was taking something out of his mouth—something made of metal. It was. . .

"Got some cake in 'ere," said Robert, glancing at the expression on my face with malicious glee as he picked tiny crumbs of cake out of the joints in his dental brace and popped them into his mouth.

As I closed my eyes in disgust, I heard the telephone in the hall 'ping' as the receiver was put down. Thank goodness for that! Relief at last! I opened my eyes as the headmaster came back into the room. Robert hastily returned his ghastly appliance to its proper place, and arranged his face in what he obviously believed to be an expression of wide-eyed innocence. It annoyed me. Why didn't he mind if I knew he wasn't innocent? What was so special about Mr. Rowley?

"Your father has arrived, Robert. I have just been speaking to him on the telephone. He asked me if you have been good lately."

Robert became very white and still. The hectic spots of colour burned even more brightly in his cheeks.

"Wot did yer say, sir?"

"I informed your father that your conduct has been as it should be, but . . . I said something else as well."

"Wot was the else, sir?"

Mr. Rowley removed his glasses and began to clean them with a soft blue cloth taken from his inside pocket.

"I told your father, Robert, that the only time I was unsure about was the period of time that passed while I was actually on the phone to him. I said that I would need to check with Mr. Harper, who is about to become a member of staff at Stapley Manor."

He replaced his glasses and frowned enquiringly at me.

"So, Mr. Harper, if you will be so kind as to furnish me with a brief report on Robert's behaviour and attitude during the last five minutes, I can decide whether or not it will be necessary to walk over to the office block and speak to Mr. Bencher again."

I was still reeling inwardly from the shock caused by Mr. Rowley's incidental reference to the success of my interview. I looked into his face, but there was only polite interest visible in his expression. I looked at Robert. Plenty visible in his expression. Panic, fear, desperate hope and pale despair. I cleared my throat.

"He—he's been very good, Mr. Rowley. Polite and, well. . . very good."

"Excellent!" beamed the headmaster. "In that case, Robert, off you go to meet your father. He will be waiting for you by the office block front door. Just one second. . ."

He brushed a few cake crumbs from Robert's pullover to the carpet.

"There! You are ready. Go!"

Robert stopped at the door and grinned at me. His teeth were crazily uneven.

"You really comin' 'ere?"

I looked at Mr. Rowley. He looked at me.

"Well, Mr. Harper? Are you err. . . coming here?"

"Yes," I replied firmly. "Yes, I think I probably am."

"You might be orlright," said Robert. Then he was gone.

Over tea, Mr. Rowley offered me the post of Housefather in the Old House in a more formal manner. I accepted, my mind in a whirl. Afterwards, he walked with me down the long drive to the lane, discussing details about moving my things into the flat, and the date on which I should start work. At the bottom of the drive he stopped and extended his hand.

"We shall see you in approximately two weeks, Mr. Harper. Mrs. Philips will write to you and confirm the details. I look forward to you joining us. Go home and prepare to be stimulated."

As I shook the headmaster's hand I felt a sudden stab of guilt about Robert.

"Mr. Rowley, there's just one thing—I told you that Robert was good for those five minutes. Well. . . he wasn't really. He was horrible. . ."

That smile again.

"Of course, Mr. Harper. Of course he was horrible. He was testing you. He will never forget how you lied for him. That was my intention in asking you to report on his behaviour while I was out of the room. I was hoping that you would not be truthful, and you did not let me down."

I felt confused.

"But, is lying. . . ?"

"Mr. Harper, Robert's father is a man who suddenly acquired a great deal of money a year or so ago. He has managed to adapt his manner and behaviour tolerably well to what he imagines to be the standards and expectations of his new neighbours and acquaintances, but young Robert has most decidely not. He just cannot be the sophisticated, middle-class boy that his father now requires."

Mr. Rowley's eyebrows rose. He bit his lip like a guilty child.

"You see, Mr. Harper, you may have distorted the truth somewhat concerning the five minutes you spent with Robert, but I spent that same period on the telephone in conversation with Mr. Bencher, Robert's father, lying through my back teeth about the boy's behaviour over the last five weeks!"

The evening following my interview was one long glow of satisfaction and happiness. There was Annie, and lots of beer, and my best friend, Steve, and Kate the delectable landlady and, best of all, there was the ever-present, sweetly precious knowledge that I had succeeded in something. Somebody had offered me a job because I had qualities that they seemed to want. Over and over again, I stroked my self-image with this thought, and for the first time for many months, it purred like a cat. I postponed any consideration of the concerns and fears that would undoubtedly erode my feelings of joy as the next fortnight passed. Why shouldn't I have just one evening when there was nothing to worry about, and no one to trouble me? Annie understood, and was wonderfully non-sensible from the moment I walked into the King's Head until the moment we walked out together at closing time giggling foolishly and waving extravagantly at Kate, who smiled indulgently at us from the bar as we left.

As we climbed up over the common towards Annie's Mount Ephraim flat, I turned and looked back at the dark mass of Tunbridge Wells, somehow picturesque even in silhouette. In two weeks time this would no longer be my home. In that moment, typically, my mood swung from elation to gloom. I noticed a wooden seat beside the path.

"Let's sit down for a minute, Annie."

"Too cold—too tired. . ." said Annie tipsily.

"Just for a moment, Annie, please."

We slumped down on the seat. I put my arm round Annie as she cuddled up against me. I gazed at the cars passing on the floodlit south-bound road below us.

"Annie," I said, "I know you're going to say I'm stupid, but I just want to be sure that my going away isn't going to make any difference to us. I couldn't stand it if—if it did."

Annie said, "You're STUPID!" and then kissed me.

Chapter Four

Moving into Stapley Manor turned out to be an uncomplicated and very pleasant experience. My gardener friend, Steve, who was as practical as I was ham-fisted, organised the hiring of a small van to transport me and my few belongings from Tunbridge Wells to Stapley. Jammed into the front of this humble vehicle, Steve, Annie and I chatted optimistically as we travelled about the job I would be starting on the following day. Steve was warmly encouraging until just before we went into the sharp bend at the south end of Mayfield when Annie happened to mention that part of the job was a responsibility for general repairs in the Old House. We very nearly crashed into the pink-emulsioned pub on the other side of the road. Steve wasn't usually a great laugher. Curly-haired, sturdy and full of common sense, a rumbling chuckle was generally about as much as he could manage. He made an exception in this case though. His roars of mirth shook the van causing it to veer off to the right as he momentarily lost control. Hauling it back on course, he spluttered a question.

"Are you seriously telling me that—that you are going to be doing the handyman bit?"

"He's fixed things for me before now," said Annie loyally.

"That's true," grinned Steve, "I know that's a fact, because I've had to fix 'em all again afterwards."

"What about the pine bookshelf I put up in my flat," I protested.

"That looked pretty good, didn't it?"

"Looked alright," said Steve. "Nice and portable too. If you got fed up with it being where it was, you only had to put a book on it and down it came!"

We all laughed. I didn't mind really. It was an old and comfortable joke that I couldn't tell a hammer from a handsaw. I just hoped George Ashton would find my unlimited incompetence equally amusing.

It felt odd to be back in Stapley. As we bucketed along the narrow High Street I just caught a glimpse of the little alley that led down to the church on the green. If Steve hadn't been there I might have taken Annie into the cool interior of St. Peter's and shown her the place where I made a final decision. I hadn't told her about the few minutes I spent in church on the day of my interview. I'd wanted to, but for some reason the experience had refused to be drawn out of its private place. I wasn't going to ask Steve to stop anyway. He had no patience with churches. I remembered that he'd once muttered something to the effect that God was too busy helping him in the garden to get involved with religion. But did that mean. . . ?

"Up here is it?"

Steve swung the wheel when I nodded and soon the heavily laden little van was screaming valiantly up Backbreak Hill, the engine gasping with relief as we finally reached the top and I was able to point out our destination. Seconds later, as we turned into the drive and chugged slowly up past the headmaster's house, Annie and I shot one, brief, desperate glance at each other. No going back now.

My flat turned out to be a very small one. Just a tiny sitting room with a sink and a Baby Belling cooker at one side, a bathroom just beside the door, and a cupboard-like bedroom almost completely filled with a single bed and a surprisingly large wardrobe. We stood in the sitting room.

"It's not very big I'm afraid, and you are rather surrounded by the boys' bedrooms, but I'm sure you'll soon settle in and. . ."

Mrs. Philips smiled with genuine warmth at Annie.

"I'm sure you'll have lots of visitors, and this room's big enough for two people to sit comfortably."

"How come the window's so big?"

Steve was standing with his back to us, looking out through the big bow window that took up almost the whole of

41

one wall. Mrs. Philips joined him, looking out over the tennis court to a magnificent view of the Downs rising guardian-like over Stapley village below us.

"Well, of course this wasn't always a school," explained the secretary. "For years it was simply a private house, built by some old Admiral I believe, and the whole of your flat, Mr. Harper, was just one of the big bedrooms."

She patted one of the side walls.

"These are new, and not terribly thick. You lose the space I'm afraid, but you do get to keep the old windows. And what could be nicer with a view like this?"

It didn't take long to move my things in. Steve and I did most of the lifting and carrying, while Annie sorted and placed and arranged and stowed away in cupboards and drawers. We had an unexpected helper. As I reached the bottom of the winding Old House back staircase a small, oddly familiar voice came piping out of the dark space under the wooden stairs.

"Mrs. Philips said I could help, sir. Please can I help? The others 've all gone out, sir. I've stayed behind to help, sir. Can I help, sir? Please can I. . . ?"

It was Dennis. After some coaxing he emerged and stood with one leg in the air and his arms wrapped over the top of his head as I introduced Steve, who shook hands gravely with the small, eager, quivering figure. Dennis would have wagged his tail furiously if he'd had one. He peered into the back of the van, eyes popping.

"I'll take it all!" he squeaked. "I'll carry every single bit, sir!"

Remembering Dennis's rather eccentric way of walking, I made sure that he set off with one or two small unbreakable objects. By the time I caught him up, he was already in the flat, bobbing happily around Annie as she arranged some fresh flowers in a milk bottle that she had purloined from a crate in the yard.

"Are you married to Miss, sir?"

I heard Steve's quiet chuckle as he came through the door behind me. Annie blushed and bent over her flowers.

"Errr. . . no, Dennis. Not—not married, no."

"But are you going to marry Miss, sir?"

Dennis's look of wide-eyed enquiry was totally innocent. I did a good imitation of a fish. Annie, still crimson, looked helplessly at Steve. Steve smile maliciously at me.

"Come on, Dave. I'd like to know the answer to that question too. Are you going to marry Miss?"

Dennis didn't get an answer to his question, but it certainly made me think. Were Annie and I going to get married one day? An hour later, when Dennis had hurried off abruptly to find someone called Mike, and Steve was waiting discreetly in the van for Annie and I to say our goodbyes, I decided to bring the subject up again. All the most important things that have happened to Annie and I seem to have cropped up on stairs of one kind or another. This was no exception. Halfway down the main Old House staircase was a flat area at the angle of the stairs. We stopped there. Through a curious porthole shaped window we could seen the van, and Steve leaning easily on the steering wheel, staring at something in the far distance. I put my arms around Annie, and studied her face carefully. I wanted to make sure I'd remember every bit of it when she'd gone. I loved her face.

"Annie, can I ask you something silly?"

"I think that would be very sensible, David."

"You know what Dennis said?"

"Yes."

"Well—what do you think?"

"What do you think?"

I chickened out.

"What do I think about what?"

Annie screwed her nose up in mock disgust. She pretended to be searching for something behind my eyes.

"David Harper! If you're in there, come out here and ask properly."

Her eyes were very soft, very deep, very grey.

"Will you marry me, Annie?"

"Yes, David, I would like to do that. Thank you for asking me."

It was as simple as that. Five minutes later they were gone, but as I watched the van make its turn round the office block at the top of the drive and disappear, I hugged Annie's 'Yes' to me like a hot water bottle, and felt very warm indeed.

It went very quiet for a while after Steve and Annie had gone. Apart from little Dennis, Mrs. Philips was the only person I had seen since we arrived. In a cardboard box on the floor by the sink I found coffee, sugar, milk and biscuits. Good old Annie. I heated some water and sat by my huge window in my tiny sitting-room, sipping coffee and listening to the silence. I thought about my second encounter with Dennis. No one had ever called me 'sir' before. Part of me couldn't help rather liking it. I would never tell anyone that of course. I would say that I couldn't care less what they called me, but one had to go along with the tradition of the place. Would all the boys call me 'sir'? A picture of the red-haired boy, Colin, thrust itself into my mind suddenly. I couldn't imagine him calling me sir. I couldn't imagine him calling anyone 'sir'. I remembered the words he'd said just before setting off with Glander in tow.

"With luck I will."

That's what I'd thought he said at the time. Since then I was pretty sure I'd worked out what he really said. Would he call me 'sir' even when he was swearing at me? Tickled by the absurdity of my own thoughts I got up and strode to and fro in the limited space, addressing myself in the pugnacious tones that I imagined Colin might use.

"Why don't you eff off, sir? You're a pain in the arse, sir! If you don't mind me sayin' so, sir, you're a bog-faced cretin! You know, sir—you really make me puke!"

I swung round and spat the final word with exaggerated venom straight into the face of Mrs. Crompton, the matron, who must have walked in through the unlatched door just at that moment.

"I'm terribly sorry to hear that, Mr. Harper. I was just going to say how pleased I am about you joining us, but. . ."

The little matron's blue eyes were twinkling, thank goodness. I wouldn't have to stumble through a ridiculously involved explanation. She sat composedly on the edge of my only armchair and smiled calmly at me.

"It's funny what we do when we're on our own—when we think we're on our own—isn't it?"

"Yes," I agreed ruefully, "it is—very funny. By the way, do you think you could call me David? I don't feel like Mr. Harper at all."

"Thank you, and my name is Ruth."

Ruth had come to welcome me officially in place of Mr. Rowley, who was away until Monday, and to make sure that I had everything I needed. She told me that, unusually, all but one of the boys were out, either at home for the weekend, or occupied with expeditions and activities in the surrounding area.

"Dennis begged to be allowed to stay in to meet you when you arrived. He said he was the first one to see you, so you'd be really upset if he wasn't here when you moved in."

My heart warmed to Dennis yet again—how nice to be wanted. I remembered something.

"Mrs. Cr—Ruth—when I came that day, Dennis told me he was a maladjusted boy. It was the first thing he said. How did he. . . ?"

The matron's face creased into a frown of exasperation.

"The stupid Council! When the school was first opened six years ago, they put a huge sign up at the bottom of the drive, informing the world—and Dennis when he first came—that this place was called Stapley Manor School for Maladjusted Boys. It took Mr. Rowley four years to persuade the geniuses higher up the ladder that it really wasn't a very clever idea. We burnt it on Guy Fawkes night two or three years ago. Boys like Tom hated and loathed it. I think it made him feel like some sort of emotional spastic. I'm sure he feels that his parents are the maladjusted ones—not him. He's probably right too. Now Dennis. . . well, to be absolutely honest he was rather pleased to discover that he was an anything. When you've been nothing all your life, I suppose even being maladjusted is a step up. Not that I imagine he has the slightest idea what it means."

I nodded slowly. Dennis and I had the same problem. I rubbed a nonexistent itch on my forehead with the flat of my hand.

"Ruth, you're going to think I'm awfully stupid, but I still don't really understand what maladjusted means."

She blinked apologetically.

"You're going to think I'm even more stupid, David, because I don't really understand what it is either. It's easier in some ways to say what it isn't."

"What isn't it, then?"

She leaned back in her chair, and studied the ceiling, eyes narrowed in thought.

"Well, it isn't like measles. It's not a nice neat disease with nice neat symptoms. In fact, it isn't an illness at all. It's certainly not mental illness, although one or two of our boys have suffered from problems of that kind. And it's definitely not backwardness or dullness of intellect. We do have a percentage of boys who are borderline educationally sub-normal, but more than half of our intake are children who could easily reach university standard. A few have been exceptionally clever—Tom, for instance. . ."

She stared into the distance, searching for a clue. We sat in silence for a few moments.

"And it's nothing to do with deliquency—bad or illegal behaviour I mean. We have our share of that, of course. You'll meet two boys in this house who have both been through the juvenile courts—Colin and Douglas. But then there are boys like Arnold Ducker and little Dennis. We'd love them to do something naughty now and then but the trust has been beaten out of them. They wouldn't dare be very bad in case we sent them away. We never would of course, but it's an uphill job persuading them of that."

My first impression of Dennis had been correct then. He had been beaten. Someone had beaten the trust out of him. The matron leaned forward, patting the tips of her fingers together. Her tone became more brisk.

"You might find some answers in the area of schooling. One thing that nearly all our boys have in common is being under-achievers. They might score very well on tests to see how they could perform, but when it comes to the performance itself they—well, they just can't do it. The other thing they all have in common is problems at home of one sort or another. Some very obvious—some much more subtle. There's an amazing variety of backgrounds just in the Old House."

She must have noticed a troubled look in my eyes.

"Don't worry, David. You'll get the hang of it eventually. You must get Mr. Rowley to tell you what he thinks about maladjustment. He's bound to say something completely different to what I've said. Anyway. . ."

Ruth patted her knees once and stood up energetically.

"If you need anything let me know. I'll be around the house all day today. And tomorrow, your first day, Mark Parish, one of our teachers, will be getting the boys up and seeing them off to school. He'll show you the ropes, and he's a lovely fellow. Just watch how he goes about things. I'll tell him to give you a knock about seven. Okay?"

As she reached the door I said, "Ruth, can I just tell you what I was doing when—when you came in just now?"

"If you want to," she smiled.

"Well, I was just imagining how Colin, the red-haired boy, would talk to a member of staff if he was in a bad temper. I was just—well, messing about really, being silly. I don't suppose he'd really say things like that."

"You're absolutely right," said Ruth as she pulled the door open. "He wouldn't say things like that. He's had a number of bad tempers with me and I can assure you that the things he says are far, far worse than that!"

Not long after my visitor had left, the sounds of folk returning began. There were shouts—mostly boyish—tramping feet echoing loudly on the stairs, occasional doors slamming, some music being played somewhere. It all sounded quite civilised and controlled, but for some reason I flicked the catch on my front door so that no one could walk in on me, and sat on the floor with my back to the door, revelling in the unusual mix of excitement and fear that tingled in my stomach.

I didn't go out of my way to meet anyone else that evening. When the hubbub had subsided to a distant hum, I assumed that tea was in progress. Creeping rather than walking down the back stairs, I hurried across the yard and down the drive. Half an hour later I was contentedly tucking into a large plate of sausages, egg and chips at the Laughing Lemming, a brightly painted cafe set between the grocers and the Post Office in Stapley High Street. From there it was a short and exquisitely enjoyable stroll to the nearest pub, a comfortable dark-panelled Victorian building called, simply, The Old Moon.

Much later, after a pleasantly weary trudge up the hill, I regained the privacy of my little flat, to find a folded piece of paper on the floor just inside the door. Humming happily, I flopped down in my armchair and unfolded the note. It was from George Ashton.

Dear Mister Harper,

Called twice to take you down and meet
the kids. Presume you're out somewhere.
Bit surprised really. Waste of opportunity,
really. Means you go in cold in the
morning.

Ashton.

Everything fell apart on the spot. Various emotions crashed
crazily around inside me. Guilt, anger, frustration and tearful
confusion chased each other up and down my mind. I should
have known it was too good to be true. No doubt George
Ashton had been the only one of the interviewing panel who
hadn't been convinced about the wisdom of appointing me. Now
this note. It wasn't fair! No one had told me I was supposed
to go down and hang around with the boys this evening. Why
should I? I wasn't officially employed until tomorrow. He had
no right to tell me what to do until then! George Ashton was
a hateful, insensitive man who shouldn't be allowed to work
with the sort of children who came to Stapley Manor. Why the
hell shouldn't I go to a pub for the evening? This stupid scrap
of paper was an insult! That's what it was—an insult!

Hard on the heels of this ridiculous hymn of self-justification
came the usual groaning truth. Why, oh why, did I always
indulge my tendency to retreat—to sit behind a locked door
- to creep quietly out and down to the pub when it made much
more sense to go and meet my new charges informally? Why
couldn't I be relaxed and spontaneous like other people?

My peace was gone.

I knew there was a cubicle near the foot of the main
stairs where the boys had access to a pay phone. I got there
without encountering anybody else and made a transfer charge
call to Annie.

"Hello, Annie. Just thought I'd call and tell you how things
are going." I knew I sounded quite casual.

"Oh. . . that's lovely, darling. Thank you. How are things
going?"

Her voice was weary but willing. She'd probably been
asleep. I kept my tone light and conversational.

"Oh, it's been okay. Had quite a good chat with the matron earlier on. Got this stupid note just now, but. . ."

"What do you mean, David? Stupid note about what?"

She was alarmed now. I could tell.

"Oh. . . just a note from George Ashton, the deputy, you know. He seemed to think it was a bit odd me going out this evening instead of staying in and meeting the Old House boys. No one told me. . ."

"But where did you go, darling?"

"What do you mean, where did I go?"

"Well, where did you go, David? Why didn't you take the chance to meet the boys? You start work with them tomorrow morning. Did you go to the pub? You went to the pub, didn't you?"

I wasn't going to get any easy comfort. My swirling feelings knotted themselves into a tight ball of fury which I flung down the receiver at Annie.

"Don't be ridiculous, Annie! I'm not in prison, am I? What right has he got to tell me what to do? I just went down to the pub for a while. That's not abnormal, is it? I certainly didn't expect to be cross-examined by you! Sometimes you make me so angry. . !"

"David, what are you. . ?"

"Oh, go away!"

I slammed the phone down, full of shame and relish. The relish lasted seconds. The same was still there when I got up at 6:00 am the next morning after a long fitful night.

"At least," I thought, as I dragged myself out of the unfamiliar bed and tried to remember where the light switch was, "I haven't slept through the alarm. They won't be able to say I'm late this morning."

With a pang I thought of Annie waking up this morning with the taste of that awful telephone conversation still in her mouth. Should I try to phone her before I started work? No, she'd apologise before I did and then I'd lose my temper again. Better to wait until my tarnished self-image had been shined up a little. I found it much easier to be genuinely magnanimous when I felt happy about myself. Not for the first time I wondered what on earth Annie saw in me. Then there was George Ashton to face at some point. As I sat on the stool in my sitting room, washed, dressed and ready for the fray, I wondered what he would say when we met. And what was this "lovely fellow" Mark Parish going to be like? Not to mention nearly fifteen maladjusted boys who I'd not yet met and who certainly weren't likely to make life any easier. I looked at my watch. Five minutes to go before I began my very first day as a housefather. Little crackles of tension tingled over my skin. I picked up the glass of orange juice that stood on the work surface beside me, and drank it back quickly. There was a quiet knock on the door.

I liked Mark Parish as soon as I saw him. From the moment I opened the door on that first morning, I don't think I ever failed to benefit in one way or another from being exposed to the atmosphere of steady humorous warmth that seemed to surround him. He must have been in his late forties, with one of those homely faces that have managed to crease in all the right places. He had a full head of thin, fluffy dark hair, spattered with flecks of grey. His voice, when he spoke, was deep and relaxed.

"My name's Mark Parish. You must be David Harper, our new housefather. Great to meet you. You're badly needed - seems an age since old Ted Boon packed his bags and walked off into the sunset."

"Ted Boon?"

"Chap before you—retired now. Good fellow. Time for a change though, I'd say."

He nodded over my shoulder towards the inside of the flat.

"Flat okay, David?"

"Oh, yes—yes it's fine. Errr. . . did you want to. . ?"

He glanced at his watch.

"Well, now, it's only just gone seven. We could fit a quick whistle-wetter in if you've got the makings here in your little kingdom. What d'you say?"

"Well, yes, if that's alright—I mean if there's nothing else we ought to be doing."

Mark Parish chuckled. He cocked his head to one side and raised a finger.

"Listen!" he said. "Can you hear that?"

I strained hard.

"I can't hear anything," I replied, fearing that even my ears were failing now.

"Quite! And you won't hear anything until I give the little boykins permission to be awake at precisely thirty minutes and one second past seven o'clock. They'll be lying there in their beds now, some of them, knowing that they have dared to wake early, and that I, Mr. M. Parish, will punish them severely if I discover their crime. And, as our main responsibility before half past seven is to ensure that noise is at a minimum and peace is at a maximum, I think we could safely risk a cuppa, don't you?"

I couldn't help laughing at this extraordinary speech. I didn't believe the bit about severe punishment at all. This man wasn't a severe punisher, but he had great natural presence. It was very difficult to imagine him being very ruffled by anything or anyone.

Mark settled contentedly in the armchair while I busied myself with tea making.

"First job with children?" he asked.

"Well, yes it is—in fact I suppose it's my first real job anywhere."

"Great!" said Mark. "Fresh approach—stir us know-alls up a bit. Easily get stale when you're a long-term fixture."

How different from Glander!

"How often do you work here in the house, Mark?"

I handed him a cup of tea.

"Ta, mate. I do three shifts a week. Most of us teachers do. It's called ex-STRAIN-eous duties! The rest of the time we're busy inflicting knowledge on the student princes, over in the classroom block. But you're the chaps who do the real work. No doubt about that."

Something about Mark's solidity and generosity of spirit made me want to confide in him. Falteringly, I described how I had arrived back the previous night to find the deputy headmaster's note waiting for me. I retrieved the screwed up piece of paper from my coffee tin waste basket and unfolded it for him to read.

"What do you think I ought to do, Mark?"

He returned the note to me, leaning back with a little smile of recognition on his face.

"That's George, alright. Not exactly an essay, is it? But look, George is a simple fellow in some ways. He's the best there is at getting close to kids like this, and if you want anything made or fixed so it stays made or fixed, then he's the man. What he's not so good at is relating to other adults for no good reason that he can see. He just doesn't bother with it. If he finds you really get stuck into working with the lads, then. . . well, he'll decide you're alright—perhaps."

I obviously didn't look very encouraged.

"Or," said Mark, "the other route to old George's heart lies straight through the middle of the woodwork room. If you're the practical sort there's no problem. He can talk bits of wood for hours on end."

I was saved from having to respond to this by Mark's sudden discovery that it was twenty-nine minutes past seven.

"Come on!" He wiped his mouth with the back of his hand and dumped his cup and saucer in the sink. "Time to move!"

Chapter Five

The next hour and a half was something of an anti-climax. Mark simply popped his head into each room that we passed, made sure that the occupant or occupants were awake, then posted himself by the bathroom and shower block at the end of the corridor to check that everyone had a wash before getting dressed. Within less than a minute after being called, the boys started to appear with their towels, a few coming downstairs from what must have once been the servants' quarters on the second floor, the majority from the larger, dormitory-like rooms on the middle corridor. They came in a variety of shapes, sizes and states. A few, presumably those who had already been awake for a time, were quite bright and light on their feet, glad to be up and about. Others, most in fact, came zombeying along the passage like little reluctant Lazaruses, clutching their blue and white striped grave clothes to them as they stumbled bleary-eyed towards the wetness. Almost all the boys managed a polite, if mumbled, greeting to Mark, who responded equally politely. It all seemed to go like clockwork. They didn't really appear to notice me.

Later, breakfast was just the same. The boys lined up in an orderly queue at the dining room door in the games room and, when Mark gave the word, filed in and settled in groups of four or five around the circular tables. Dennis bobbed frantically at me from a table by the window, patting the seat beside him and beckoning with one fiercely flapping hand. I very much enjoyed the near-ecstasy with which he greeted my decision to join him. It made me feel that I belonged. I noticed that a seat had been reserved next to Colin, the red-haired boy, for Mark, who accepted it with the same pleasant gravity that he had shown towards the boys since thirty minutes and one second past seven. I was amazed by how effortless it all was. When everyone was settled, Mark spoke in a quiet, deep voice.

"Let's say grace, please."

A hush descended as the simple grace was said, followed by a scraping of chairs as servers from each table collected bowls of cereal from a hatch in the wall, returning a little later for plates, each containing a slice of toast and a sausage. Dennis was the server on our table. There was no argument about it, not even a brief discussion. The other two boys on my table said hardly a word throughout breakfast. One was a short, very round boy with little gleaming eyes and a quite incredible capacity for bread and butter which was available in huge piles on each table to supplement the main meal. My conversation with him was not a great success.

"Are you enjoying your bread and butter?"

"Yes."

"Good! Do you err. . . always have bread and butter?"

"Yes."

"Good! That's good, because that means you've got err. . . something to—to enjoy, haven't you?"

"Yes."

"Would you like me to pass you some more, or. . ?"

"Yes."

I gave up.

The other boy was a little older, with neat hair and a rather stern, studious look about him. He addressed me just after the cereal stage in one of those raspy, mid-adolescent schoolboy voices.

"Are you a new member of staff, sir?"

"Yes, that's right. I am, yes. . ."

"Are you here instead of Mr. Boon, sir?"

"Yes, I suppose I am. I'm the housefather for the Old House."

"Are you strict, sir?"

I considered this. Should I claim to be strict? What precisely did he mean by the term? Would being strict mean a greater chance of inspiring the right blend of respect and liking? Or not?

I looked across at Mark, chatting quietly to Colin, who seemed much milder than I remembered him. I hadn't heard Mark so much as raise his voice all morning. He certainly wasn't strict. I decided to take my cue from him.

"No," I said, "I'm not strict. I think it's better just to be friendly."

I smiled as agreeably as I could. A deep shuddering sigh went through the studious looking boy. The gleam in the little fat boy's eyes shone more brightly. Dennis started talking about hedgehogs. I wasn't sure what was going on, but they were all behaving well so I wasn't too troubled.

When the meal was finished, Mark rose to his feet, took a piece of paper from his pocket, and read out a list of domestic tasks together with the names of boys allocated to each. There were things like boot room tidying, hoovering, sweeping, bathroom cleaning and litter collection. The group dispersed chattily to get on with their various jobs. I followed Mark as he strolled casually out into the yard, where two of the Old House boys were sweeping one half of the expanse of tarmac between the school block and the houses. Mark pointed across the yard.

"Imagine a line between the middle of the bottom step and the middle of the kitchen. Everything to the left of that line is down to us. Sweeping—litter—whatever."

I was very impressed. The two sweepers were extraordinarily precise and thorough. Soon there was a long narrow path of dust and litter across the centre of our section. This was swept into a large central pile and disposed of with quiet efficiency. Over to my right I noticed a boy emerge from a door that opened on to the yard from the New House. He was tall and thin—even thinner than me. He gave his section of the yard a couple of perfunctory pokes with his brush, then leaned on the handle as though overcome by unutterable weariness. Finally, he turned and dragged himself back into the building, trailing the brush dismally behind him. I couldn't help feeling a little flash of pride. Our part of the yard was spotless. Theirs was a mess. That boy hadn't even tried!

I followed Mark round the house as he toured the completed tasks. The boys seemed pleased when he praised them, and only mildly resentful when he pointed out bits they'd missed or not worked quite hard enough on. After shoe cleaning and room tidying, the boys lined up once more—at the foot of the classroom block steps this time.

"Time for assembly," explained Mark, as he indicated to the front boy to lead on into the school.

Along the corridor we marched and through some swing doors into a gymnasium at the far end, where the boys sat themselves cross-legged on the floor in rows facing a lectern at one end, behind which George Ashton was standing. He nodded very briefly at me without smiling. Mark organised one boy into giving out song-books, then strolled over and talked quietly to the deputy, while I leaned against the wallbars at the side feeling rather uncomfortable. Seconds later I was distracted by a noise travelling along the corridor towards us. It was a loud, riotous sort of noise, made up of shouting, scuffling, running feet, and a loud adult voice imploring and threatening by turns as the whole caravan of confusion came closer and closer. The swing doors crashed open at last and the New House boys started to come in. It was as though a magical transformation occurred as each boy passed through the door. Whatever they might have been in the corridor, they were models of decorum once they entered the gym. Maybe it had something to do with the way in which George Ashton, who'd broken off his conversation with Mark, was giving each newcomer a very straight look indeed. Once again I felt that sense of pride. How fortunate I was to have ended up in the Old House and not with this rabble who had just come in. Our boys had made very little noise in the corridor.

The last person in the line was a harassed-looking young man who couldn't have been much older than me. He was one of those bear-like characters, not tall, and broad without being fat. He wore a big fluffy dark pullover, and a full black beard.

Mark, who had joined me by the wallbars, leaned towards my ear.

"Mike Merry," he whispered. "Teacher. Does all the Biology and Rural Studies and suchlike. Kids love him. Great chap."

I didn't doubt that he was a great chap. But he wasn't a very happy chap on this particular morning. He looked as if he'd just fought a particularly intense battle—and lost. Red faced and breathless, he took up his stance against the wallbars on the opposite side to me, and glared at his charges. I noticed Tom sitting in the middle of one row.

Other people came in during the next minute or two, the rest of the teaching force I presumed, and finally Ruth Crompton slipped in apologetically, smiled warmly at me, and stood beside and slightly behind George Ashton who was clearly anxious to open proceedings. No sign of A.E. Rowley. I wondered where he was.

Assembly consisted of a prayer, a hymn, a short but unexpectedly sweet talk by the deputy headmaster, another hymn and a final prayer. It all went very smoothly, and afterwards, as the boys disappeared class by class with their teachers, I wondered why I had ever worried about this job. Soon, there was only Ruth Crompton and I left in the gym. She stood beside me as the last of the boys let the swing doors flap back into position behind him.

"Well, David, what do you think?"

I shook my head incredulously.

"It's amazing, Ruth! It all went so easily this morning."

"Ah, well, it doesn't always. . ."

"I mean, when you consider how difficult nearly all of these boys could be, it's—well, it's quite amazing."

"You reckon Mark handled them pretty well then?"

"They didn't need any handling really, Ruth. Mark didn't have to do anything. It all just—happened."

"Mmmm. . ."

Ruth looked as if she was about to say something else but she seemed to change her mind. She pushed the doors open and we walked slowly along the corridor. When we came out onto the steps at the other end, she stopped and turned to me.

"What are you going to do for the rest of the day, David?"

I fished in my pocket for the timetable that Mr. Rowley had given me before I left on the day of my interview and studied it for a moment.

"Well," I said, "according to this I go on working now for another hour and a half until ten-thirty, then I'm off until four o'clock, then back on until the boys have gone to bed. I suppose I ought to be going and fixing something or other now."

Ruth laughed out loud at the doleful expression on my face.

"No," she said firmly. "Not today! No fixing today. If Mr. Rowley had been here I know he was intending to have a chat with you this morning about all sorts of things. He's held up in London this morning and, as George is busy teaching, that means I'm in charge at the moment. So—my orders are as follows. . ."

"Yes?" I asked, rather uneasily.

"You're to go along to Mrs. Murchison in the kitchen. . ."

"Yes. . ?"

"And you're to say that Mrs. Crompton said. . ."

"Mmmm. . ?"

"Would she kindly put together a packed lunch for Mr. Harper. . ."

"A packed lunch?"

"That's right," said Ruth definitely. "Then—you are to take your packed lunch and get out on these beautiful hills of ours. You don't need to be back until four. You'll be joining Mark again. . . Well? Is that okay? Or am I bullying you too much?"

It was marvellous, and so exactly what I needed at that moment. It seemed all wrong somehow. I said so, but Ruth was adamant. It was just right, she said. Over the coming months, I was to discover that Ruth Crompton had a remarkable talent for knowing what was "just right" for all sorts of people—children and adults.

I had a blissful few hours up on top of the world. At the end of a lengthy walk I found an attractive little pub hidden in a hollow in the hills, and supplemented my packed lunch with a refreshing pint of the locally brewed bitter. By the time I found my way back to Stapley Manor I was feeling richly content and actively looking forward to the remainder of my first working day.

Mark was as calm and genial as he had been earlier, despite the fact that he was launching into the last lap of a very long day. I watched as he distributed pocket-money to a few of the boys who were going down to Stapley between end of school and teatime. Some of the lads, Colin and his sidekick Douglas in particular, asked for quite large amounts. Mark persuaded them gently but firmly that they would be wiser to take less. They grumbled a little as they left, but both boys were back in good time for tea, which turned out to be almost as uneventful as breakfast. My table seemed a little louder than the others for some reason, but I assumed it was just extra high spirits after a day of being confined in classrooms. Everything else was just the same. Dennis did the serving, the fat boy ate mountains of bread and butter, and the studious boy (who turned out to be the Arnold Ducker that Ruth had mentioned) sat with a wrinkled brow, occasionally producing long complicated descriptions of obscure mathematical work he'd been occupied with earlier in the day. Neither of the other two boys made the slightest response to his loud schoolboyish voice and I didn't understand what he was talking about, but he didn't seem to mind particularly.

After tea Mark sat everybody down in the TV room and sorted out expeditions and activities for the evening. I ended up playing 'Cheat' with Dennis and Arnold. It was a less than satisfactory experience because both of them found it almost impossible to cheat without feeling guilty. Arnold blushed heavily each time he put down cards that were not what he claimed them to be and Dennis said things like, "Two kings—but not really!"

The only other major event of the evening was supper, prepared by Colin and Douglas in the big kitchen and consisting of a cup of soup and a roll and butter. Dennis and Arnold collected theirs from the hatch and brought it back to the dining room table where we continued with our card game until bedtime. Once, Robert appeared in the dining room covered in soup stains and breadcrumbs. He left his mug on the hatch and wandered over to our table, a grin of recognition etched unevenly across his pale face.

"Di'n't recernise yer, sir! 'Syou innit, sir?"

I was pleased. I'd wondered why Robert hadn't seemed to notice me earlier. Now, as I watched him peering at me through his thick glasses, I realised that he probably hadn't even seen me.

"Yes, Robert," I admitted, "it's me. I'm your housefather now."

Robert looked puzzled.

"Where's Boon then?"

I was amazed. Surely Robert must have been told that Mr Boon had left. Perhaps it just hadn't sunk in.

"Mr. Boon's left, Robert. He's gone. I've taken his place."

59

A look of real alarm spread over the boy's face.

"Mista Rowley's not gorn 'as 'e, sir?"

I hastened to reassure Robert that Mr. Rowley had not 'gorn'. The smile came back.

"Tha's orlright then! Just Spoony-Boony gorn then. See yer, sir."

At nine o'clock I followed Mark into the TV room where he switched off the television and indicated by a jerk of the thumb that it was time for bed. Over the following half hour I watched as my colleague strolled from bedroom to bedroom checking that everyone had washed, chatting quietly to the boys as they sat up in bed reading or drawing. It all seemed very civilised. I lingered for a few moments in Dennis' room. He occupied one of the beds in a double room. The other bed was empty. All I could see of Dennis was a pair of bright eyes and a wisp of hair sticking out at the top of the covers.

"G'night, sir," said the small muffled voice. "Am I good at Cheat, sir?"

"Err. . . yes, Dennis," I replied untruthfully, "You're very good—well, just as good as Arnold anyway."

Dennis cleared his throat.

"Do you like me, sir?"

"Yes," I said, slightly embarrassed, "of course I like you, Dennis. I like you very much."

It was so easy to say. I wondered if it really meant anything to this battered little person. I switched the light out and found Mark down on the lower corridor. He joined me for a quick coffee in the flat, and then left to drive home down the hill into Stapley.

As I stood by my window watching the lights of Mark's car as it threaded its way between the hedges of the lane, I felt pretty good. I knew I would be able to sleep well tonight. But first, I wanted to make my peace with Annie. Now it was clear that the job wasn't going to present me with control problems I was feeling much more relaxed. All I had to do now was ring Annie and say sorry. After that everything would be alright. The business with George Ashton could wait until tomorrow when I had a chance to speak to him and explain about last night. I'd sort it out somehow. I tiptoed downstairs.

It was some time before Annie answered the phone.

"Hello—is that you, David?"

"Yes, Annie, it's me. Look, I'm. . ."

"You're sorry! Right?"

"Yes, that's what I was just about to. . ."

"You're a selfish sod sometimes, David Harper. You've woken me up tonight just like you woke me up last night. I'm too tired to play silly games. And there's no point in ringing me up just so that you can tell me to go away. One of these days I might do just that and then who'd untangle your knotted entrails for you? Huh? Who?"

"I really enjoyed today, Annie. I think I'm going to like it here."

"Good. I'm very glad, David. What about Mr. Whatsit? Have you seen him?"

I gave Annie a brief description of my first day's work, and assured her that my entrails were all in order. By the time I put the phone down all was well. I would see her next week in Tunbridge Wells. That would be marvellous. I'd look forward to that. Half an hour later I was in bed, and fast asleep.

Chapter Six

"Go on, sir! Just another quarter of an hour! Mr. Boon always used to let us."

"Yeah! Please, sir. We'll go to bed as soon as the programme finishes."

"It's not fair, sir! Mr. Boon never minded. . ."

"We liked Mr. Boon, sir. . ."

"Go on, sir. . ."

I subsided miserably into my chair at the back of the Old House television room. I was nearing the end of my first day of working with the boys on my own, and I wasn't very happy about the way things were going. I should have just switched off the TV at nine o'clock and ignored the chorus of protests, but the events of the past few hours had weakened my confidence. I felt soft and flabby inside as I waited in the near-darkness for the programme to finish and the final challenge of bedtime to begin. All morning and evening I had been feebly attempting to assert my authority over what now seemed an appallingly behaved gang of little savages. Each time, the legendary, apparently superhuman figure of Mr. Boon, my predecessor, had been held up and quoted by the boys as a perfect example of the ideal housefather. They were at pains to make it quite clear that next to this paragon, I emerged as a humourless, authoritarian dullard who was intent on making their lives as unhappy as possible. As I stared unseeingly at the big black and white screen at the other end of the room, I thought how much I would enjoy throttling the God-like Boon who seemed to have combined deep natural authority with almost supernatural understanding and compassion. Next to him I felt very pale and insubstantial indeed.

The programme, which had seemed eternal, was finishing. I waited. Another programme began. One or two of the more timid boys flicked the briefest of glances over their shoulders in my direction. It was the only indication of the mass exodus that should have begun. Why hadn't they all got up and gone to bed? Horrified by this corporate act of treachery, I rose tensely to my feet, and squeezed my way round the side of the room until I was standing beside the television set raised up on its big wooden easy-viewing stand. My mouth was dry and leathery as I reached out to switch off the set. I searched feverishly in my mind for something dynamic to say—something that would not only express the anger and disappointment I felt, but also inspire the kind of respect and admiration that had been sadly lacking since the beginning of this awful day. It was a tall order. The first groans began as my fingers touched the volume switch.

"Oh, sir! That's not fair. . ."

"Mr. Boon wouldn't have. . ."

"Just another few minutes, sir!"

"We'll go to bed straight away. . ."

"Mr. Boon was nice. . ."

They say you learn by your mistakes. I should have remembered that the only source of light in that room for the last hour had been the TV screen. As I turned the switch to 'Off' the room was plunged into darkness. The ensuing silence lasted for about half a second. Thereafter, all I could hear from the abyss before me was the crashing of chairs and assorted squeals and shouts as most of the boys took delighted advantage of my lack of foresight. The light switch was at the other end of the room near the door. To reach it I would have to wade through a mass of heaving bodies and furniture. That would make the situation ten times worse. What on earth should I do? What would the amazing Boon have done? I could shout at the top of my voice but would they listen? I could switch the television back on, but that would mean I'd given in yet again. In the dark, alone and indecisive, I felt a childlike whimper rising in me as the level of noise and confusion rose to a disturbing pitch.

I just couldn't understand it. Yesterday, when Mark had been in charge, it had all looked so easy. Why was it all so different when I was the only adult around?

I had started my second working day in a very optimistic frame of mind. I was rather looking forward to setting the morning machinery into motion, then standing back to watch from a purely supervisory point of view. While I burnt myself a slice of toast on the Baby Belling, my mind was playing with the pleasant picture of Annie, impressed beyond measure, when she first witnessed the casual way in which I handled this bunch of difficult kids. I chuckled at the thought as I threw my charred failure into the bin and glanced at my watch. Seven-thirty. Abandoning the idea of a cooked breakfast I hurried into the corridor, closed the door carefully behind me, and began to tour the bedrooms one by one calling out a cheerful greeting, and stopping only to make sure that eyes were open or bodies stirring—just as Mark had done. Within two or three minutes I had covered both corridors and was back down by the shower block, ready for the first wave of pyjamaed figures to arrive for their ablutions. Leaning easily against the doorway I thought about the next few days. Mr. Rowley would probably be around today. Perhaps I'd get the chance to have a chat with him. I'd take Ruth's advice and ask him how he would define maladjustment. The other thing I really wanted to do was climb up to the top of the Peak. maybe I could get two or three of the boys together, Dennis and Robert and one or two others, say. We could go and play games up there, then Dennis could roll down and be sick. We might even go up there one night with a primus stove and cook some sausages. That would be great fun. If the school had some tents in that camp store that Tom had pointed out to me, we might even spend a few nights. . .

These pleasant reflections were cut short abruptly by two things. The first was the sudden appearance of a boy from the bedroom at the end of the corridor. He was fully dressed, thoroughly dishevelled and patently unwashed. He shambled towards me, scratching his head with both hands as he came.

The second was my awareness that I had been standing by the shower block for nearly five minutes and that this human wreck lurching along the passage in my direction was the only person who had responded to my early-morning call. And he hadn't washed! My watch showed that it was nearly twenty to eight. By this time yesterday, more than half of the boys had stumbled in for their washes. What was going wrong?

The boy, a tallish, well-built lad of about fifteen, was obviously not about to waste any energy on speaking to me. He continued his neanderthal shuffle straight past me towards the top of the back stairs. I cleared my throat in his direction. He stopped, turned round, pushed a few greasy strands of black hair away from his eyes and focussed on me for the first time.

"What?"

"Errr. . . you haven't actually washed, have you?"

His stare was totally impassive.

"So?"

"Well—you're supposed to, aren't you?"

"Who says?"

I swallowed hard.

"Yesterday, when Mr. Parish was on. . ."

For the first time alarm flickered across the sleepily arrogant expression on the boy's face.

"Is Mr. Parish on with you?"

"Well, no he isn't, but. . ."

"Thought not. He's off. Boon never made me wash."

To my intense annoyance, the boy turned away and started to descend the stairs, obviously feeling that further discussion was superfluous. I was furious! How dare he speak to me like that? How dare he treat me as if I didn't count? Good heavens - he wasn't even calling me 'sir'!

"Just a moment!"

The boy stopped on the second stair and sighed like one whose patience is unbearably stretched. He turned his head as if it was a wearisomely heavy weight to move.

"What?"

"I'm not Mr. Boon!"

"Nor am I," said the boy, without pausing for even a fraction of a second. For a moment I was nonplussed. Was this cheek, or logic, or maladjustment—or what?

"What I mean is that Mr. Boon may not have made you wash, but I am not Mr. Boon, and I am going to make you wash!"

"You're going to make me wash, are you?"

A slight sound made me swing round at that moment. Six or seven pyjamaed forms had materialised in the corridor and were frozen in attitudes of enjoyable anticipation as my confrontation with the lank-haired boy neared its climax. I turned back towards the stairs with a heavy heart. If I lost this battle in front of all these boys, no one would ever do anything I told them again.

"Yes!" I said, with a confidence that was one hundred per cent counterfeit "If I have to I'll make you."

There was more than a hint of Clint Eastwood in my tone but then I had no other model on which to draw. The 'baddie' on the stairs narrowed his eyes still further as he tried to assess the odds. It was an unspeakably horrible, tension-ridden moment, and it was real life. Baddies could win in real life. To my immense relief the boy finally dropped his gaze and, mumbling an unintelligible insult, slouched past me into the shower block. He turned a tap on with one vicious flick of the wrist and, bending over the wash basin, splashed a few drops of water in the general direction of his face. Without bothering to towel himself he stomped out past me and disappeared round a bend in the stairs, calling out just one word as he went.

"Satisfied?"

I leaned against the wall, suddenly weak after my ordeal. At least I hadn't totally failed.

"We're not allowed to wash with our clothes on, sir. You should've made him put his pyjamas back on and then had a wash, sir. He's got away with it, sir."

Incensed, I rounded on Arnold Ducker. All the anger and frustration that I had felt towards the lank-haired boy was vented on Arnold, whose saw-blade voice had rasped through my uneasy satisfaction.

"If you spent more time washing yourself and less time telling other people where they've gone wrong, you wouldn't be such a stupid little boy!"

This crass, meaningless speech sent little Dennis, who'd been standing behind Arnold, rushing wildly into the shower block, where he started to wash frenziedly until he became a mere blur of flailing arms and water spray. Every few seconds he stopped and glanced fearfully at me to check that I'd noticed how busy he was. Glancing back at Arnold, I saw to my horror that two large tears had rolled out of his eyes and were slowly dribbling down the sides of his nose. The other boys were drifting into the shower block, muttering as they went about how I'd "made Arnold cry," and asking why I couldn't be nice like Mr. Boon. Arnold wiped his eyes with a pyjama sleeve.

"I'm sorry I said that about you letting Martin Jarrold off, sir. I wasn't trying to be rude. . ."

There was a pathetic catch in the big, awkward voice. From the shower block a different, disembodied voice rose above the sounds of splashing and chatter.

"You're a blasted bully, Harper!"

Everything in me seemed to die. I'd only been working on my own for fifteen minutes and my dignity was in ruins. I pretended I hadn't heard those awful words.

"It's not your fault, Arnold. I'm sorry I got angry with you. I just. . ."

"Can I get washed now please, sir?"

"Yes, Arnold," I gestured dismally towards the showers. "Carry on and get washed."

He stopped in the doorway. My nerves stood to attention once more.

"Colin and Douglas haven't even got up yet, sir, and it's nearly ten to eight, sir."

Would this nightmare never end? I wanted to strangle Arnold all over again. I gritted my teeth.

"Alright, Arnold. I'll see to that—you just get washed."

I ran up the little narrow staircase and strode along the shorter top corridor to the double room at the end which Colin and Douglas shared. All that could be seen of Colin was his hair, unnaturally vivid against the white pillow. Douglas was completely hidden under a mound of bedclothes. I looked at my watch. Seven-fifty exactly. I'd show these two. I took a deep breath and shouted at the top of my voice.

"If you two aren't up and dressed in two minutes flat you will be for it!"

My heart nearly stopped beating as the two inert forms seemed to explode out of their beds into a vertical position. Both were fully dressed.

"Surprise, surprise!" they chorussed, then collapsed back onto their beds shouting with laughter.

My own shout was still echoing in my ears. What a fool! Why hadn't I checked? Still, at least they were up and dressed - hold on though, they hadn't washed! They couldn't have been down to the shower block. I'd have seen them. My heart sank. For a moment I was tempted to pretend that I thought they'd washed, it would be so much easier. But this was my first day on my own. Tomorrow. . .

"Very funny, Colin and Douglas, but you haven't washed yet. You can just get back into your pyjamas and have a wash like all the rest."

Colin's laughter stopped dead. Some sort of quick-boiling mechanism seemed to suffuse his face and even his hair with the very colour of fury. He thrust his face into mine, his top lip curled in sneering aggression.

"Who SAYS we haven't washed?"

My blood sank to my boots.

"I say you haven't washed, and if. . ."

"You calling me a piggin' liar. . .?"

Time for my ace card. I controlled the slight tremor that threatened to rob my words of all authority.

"I've been down by the shower block since half-past seven, and neither you nor Douglas have come down the stairs—let alone washed. So—yes! If you like, I am calling you a liar! What else can I think?"

Douglas, fair haired and much cooler than Colin, a sort of small scale Steve McQueen, had a very unpleasant glint in his eye as he spoke for the first time.

"Look, 'e's gone all white an' trembly. 'E's scared. You wanna smack 'im in the mouth, Col. Teach 'im some manners. Boon wouldn't've called us liars. 'E was alright, old Boon was, not like this pratt!"

For one terrible moment I very nearly burst into tears. There was an evilly sharp edge on Douglas' comments that flayed great strips of skin off my self-esteem and left me raw.

"Have you ever kept a hedgehog as a pet, sir?"

The crazy intrusion of little Dennis' question, into such a fraught situation, created a mild hysteria in me for a moment. I laughed mirthlessly as I glanced over my shoulder at the small earnest figure.

"I'll be with you in a moment, Dennis. Hold on a sec."

As I turned back again, I realised with some surprise that a strong and very steady reaction had replaced the emotional collapse that I'd feared. I moved aside from Colin and spoke directly and very quietly into Douglas' face. I held up an index finger.

"If you ever, ever speak to me like that again, I shall make absolutely sure that you are very, very sorry, Douglas. I hope you won't be that stupid."

It was Douglas' turn to go pale. His eyes, intelligent and calculating, read in mine a primitive determination to protect myself when it came to the final crunch. He forced a one-sided smile onto his face.

"Only jokin', sir. Sorry."

He hadn't been joking and he wasn't sorry, just expedient. I told myself that I would never make the mistake of trusting Douglas. Colin was made of much simpler stuff. He inserted himself into my eyeline again.

"Are you still saying we haven't washed? Because we piggin' well have washed!"

"Colin," I said, shaking my head with impatience, "how can you have washed without coming downstairs and passing me at the door of the shower block?"

"They used that wash basin over there, sir," piped Dennis' voice cheerily from behind me. "They're the only ones who've got one in their room, sir."

I screwed my eyes tight shut then opened them wide again. Dennis was right. There was a wash basin at the side of the room. I hadn't noticed it yesterday morning, and I certainly hadn't noticed it just now.

"Ah!" I said feebly. "Yes. . . right, I see—right. You used. . . errr. . . right."

I felt filleted.

"I'm sorry, Colin. I was wrong. You have washed. I didn't realise."

"Told yer!" Colin was triumphant.

"Can we go down for breakfast now, sir?"

Douglas' strategic politeness was not as intimidating as his abuse, but it came pretty close.

"Yes," I said. "You can go down and queue for breakfast. Off you go."

The two boys walked off down the corridor towards the stairs, Colin swaggered and laughing, Douglas quiet-footed and restrained. He looked back at me once, a strange, disguised threat in his eyes.

"You comin', sir?" said Dennis.

"Yes, Dennis. We'd better go."

I looked at my watch. It was eight o'clock. I'd only been working for half an hour and I felt as if I'd been through a car-crusher. A thought suddenly struck me.

"Just a moment, Dennis. Wait there just a moment. . ."

I slipped quickly back into Douglas and Colin's room, and ran my hand round the inside of the wash basin.

It was bone dry.

The rest of the morning was entirely consistent with the first half hour. When I got downstairs at last I found that the queue for breakfast consisted of only two boys, Arnold Ducker and Dennis. The others were already sitting at their tables attacking the piles of bread and butter in front of them. When I objected, about ten voices informed me loudly that Mr. Boon always let them go straight into breakfast without lining up and that he never bothered to say grace. I repeated that I was not Mr. Boon, and that I would be expecting them to line up every morning when I was working, and that we would say grace before the meal. Breakfast itself was chaos. The level of noise was appalling, food was once or twice thrown across the room, and a fight broke out on Colin's table after Colin had accused Martin Jarrold of combing dandruff into his cornflakes. It was at this point, when Martin Jarrold had two firm handholds on Colin's hair and was about to head-butt him scientifically right between the eyes, and a small boy on the next table was making constant low mooing noises like a cow, and Robert was dropping wet cereal bowls into each other to see what sort of noise it made, and most of the others were shouting at the tops of their voices to make themselves heard, that I decided I'd had enough. Picking up my own cereal bowl by it's rim, I banged it down on the table as hard as I could. It certainly did the trick. It stopped the noise completely. It also smashed the cereal bowl into several pieces. As the last piece rocked to a standstill on the floor, Martin Jarrold released his grip on Colin's scalp, the mooer halted in mid moo, and Robert gently placed the last cereal bowl on top of the pile in front of him. There was a dramatic silence.

"You have to write that down in the breakage book, sir. Bowls are fifty pence, sir."

Arnold will never know how drastically his life expectancy was reduced at that moment. I gritted my teeth.

"Thank you, Arnold. I'm not concerned about that just now. I'm concerned about the disgraceful behaviour that I've been forced to sit and watch ever since breakfast began. I have never. . ."

Robert interrupted.

"Old Boony never minded. . ."

"I don't give a twopenny damn what Mr. Boon did or did not mind! I am not Mr. Boon and I do mind. Breakfast is finished whether you've finished or not. Clearers can stay and tidy up, the rest of you get on with your jobs!"

Morosely, angrily, muttering abuse in stage whispers, the boys trailed out and dispersed to various parts of the house. That same disembodied voice that had sworn at me from the shower block earlier sounded from some hidden corner again.

"Why does the Old House get all the crap stuff? At least Boon used to let us eat!"

I hadn't the heart to follow up the voice and discipline it's owner. I wandered out into the yard, gloomily reflecting that at least the sweepers knew their job. The sight that met me when I got there was like a strange inversion of the morning before. The two boys who had done such a smart and efficient job yesterday were languidly stabbing the ground with their brushes while on the New House side, the tall thin boy who had appeared to be almost expiring at the end of his brush last time I had seen him, was working energetically and methodically across his area, doing a superb job. Summoning up my last reserves of courage and conscience, I called my two sweepers over. They were pleasant-featured boys, whose names I didn't yet know. Both were about thirteen or fourteen.

"Look, lads. Yesterday you did a great job on this yard. Today you're not trying."

"Mr. Boon. . ."

Something in my face must have indicated that this was not a profitable line to pursue. I spoke again.

"I just want you to do the same job today as you did yesterday, alright?"

"And you'll check it will you, sir?" said the smaller boy whose straight brown hair seemed to have been cut by the old pudding basin method.

"Yes," I said. "I'll check it."

"Mr. Boon never used to check jobs, sir," said the other one, "so it didn't seem. . . dunno really."

"You do a good job," I promised, "and I'll come and check every bit of it, okay?"

"Yes, sir!" said the older boy, apparently newly inspired. "Come on, Tim, let's do it extra well!"

It was my first really positive encounter of the morning, and it momentarily lifted my spirits. The feeling didn't last long. As I walked around the house inspecting the other jobs, I realised that little or no effort had been expended on them. I spent the whole of the remaining half hour before assembly finding those responsible and coaxing or threatening them into doing the work that they had done so easily and co-operatively yesterday. Some I frankly chickened out of. I pretended not to notice that the upper corridor (Colin and Douglas' job) was clearly unswept. I 'forgot' to check that the boot room had been cleaned and tidied by Martin Jarrold. After all, I told myself, you can only survive so many confrontations in one morning.

By nine o'clock a ragged, bickering line of boys had formed up by the classroom steps, ready for assembly. All of them seemed vaguely untidy. Some pairs of shoes were not cleaned. The very air between them was heavy with bad feeling and dissatisfaction. The small fat boy who sat on Dennis and Arnold's table was a picture of resentful misery at the end of the line.

"You wait till my dad hears we weren't allowed to have any breakfast," he muttered at me, his little eyes black with annoyance, "then you'll be in trouble. At least Mr. Boon never. . ."

"Lead on!" I called to the front boy, who promptly tripped over the bottom step and started to scream as two or three bodies landed on top of him as the queue pushed forward.

"Stand still!" I bawled. "Stand still and for goodness sake, shut up!"

A few moments later the line of boys, still laughing and shouting despite my attempts to restore order, were tramping loudly down the corridor towards the gym where, thankfully, they underwent the same magical transformation as the New House boys had done yesterday. At the end of the assembly I didn't wait around to speak to anyone. I didn't want to see or hear anybody for a while. I just wanted to be in my own place—on my own. I regained the safety of the flat without bumping into another human being and, with a deep sigh of profound relief, shut and locked the door and dropped like a sack of potatoes into my chair.

The doorbell rang immediately.

It was a middle-aged lady dressed in a flowery housecoat and carrying a mop and bucket. There was a mixture of irritation and satisfaction in her expression. Her voice was flat, her tone sardonic.

"Mr. 'Arper?"

"Yes, that's right. I'm Mr. Harper. What can I. . . ?"

"I 'ope you're not expectin' me to make all them beds on that top landin', because I ain't!"

I stared.

"Errr. . . I'm sorry—I don't think we've been. . ."

'I've never done 'em before an' I ain't doin' 'em now!"

"I'm sorry, Mrs. . ."

"'Oo's goin' to make 'em? That's what I wanna know!"

"Well. . ."

"They're s'posed to be done after breakfast, or so I've always been told. Mrs. Crompton's words to me in the past were 'Don't you touch them beds, Mrs. Gage. Them's the boys' responsibility.' Very clear she was about that. So 'oo's gonna do 'em?"

I sighed wearily.

"I'll make them, Mrs. Gage. I'll go and make them right now. Alright?"

73

"Just as long as I'm not expected to do 'em," replied the cleaning lady, who had obviously been looking forward to a much longer and more heated discussion on the matter. "Only it's not right that I should be expected to do it when Mrs. Crompton said. . ."

"Right!" I interrupted, "You're absolutely right! I'm doing them. Me. Not you. Here I go, walking away to do them. Right?"

My heavy sarcasm, born out of frustration and quite out of character really, was completely wasted on Mrs. Gage. As I mounted the stairs at the far end of the corridor, I could hear her still muttering to herself.

"I don't see why I should do it. Mrs. Crompton said. . ."

Douglas and Colin could have taken a few lessons in swearing from me as I sweated from room to room on the top corridor, trying to bring order out of the chaos of bedclothes, pyjamas and yesterday's dirty clothes that seemed to have been almost deliberately strewn around in the most untidy fashion possible. It took me more than half an hour to sort the three bedrooms out, but at last it was done and I turned to leave the room nearest to the top of the stairs. Standing in the doorway was George Ashton.

I hate it when I blush. Some people just go slightly pink when they are embarrassed. I become red hot. I glow like the bars on an electric fire. I want to die on the spot. I wanted to die now as the deputy headmaster looked from me to the beds, and from the beds back to me. His granular features registered annoyance and scorn.

"I came over to talk about repairs, Mr. Harper, but I see you're busy making beds. The boys are supposed to do that, you know."

"I know that, Mr. Ashton. It's just that it was my first morning on my own and I didn't get round to checking the top corridor for some reason. It was all confusing and they were being difficult and I wasn't quite sure. . ."

"You were on with Mark yesterday, weren't you?" cut in the deputy uncompromisingly. "Didn't you watch what he did?"

"Yes," I said. "But he made it all look so easy. I never realised. . ."

My voice trailed off miserably.

"Well, anyway—you've got some things to fix. Here's the list. Tools in the woodwork room."

George Ashton laid a piece of paper on the radiator under the window and stomped off down the stairs without further comment. I knew that he regarded me as an incompetent ninny, and at that moment I felt quite certain that he was absolutely right.

I draw a veil over my first ignominious attempts to repair locker doors and wardrobe shelves. The results were laughable. Nor do I care to remember in detail the period between school and tea when Colin stood in the middle of the courtyard outside, yelling at the top of his voice that Harper was a "piggin' thief!" because I wouldn't allow him to withdraw all his pocket money at one go. Tea would have made one of those mediaeval feasts look like a vicar's tea party, and the rest of the evening was a nightmare of confrontations, frantic counting of heads to make sure that no one had run away, and a wild supper-time which ended with soup and crisps all over the dining room floor. In addition, I discovered that Martin Jarrold had forced Arnold Ducker to give him his supper in exchange for a topless biro that had run out of ink. This time Martin came very close to hitting me, but again he backed down at the last moment and Arnold regained his supper. It was only when the whole group settled in the TV room to watch an American detective programme that I was able to relax for the first time, knowing that the next thing to happen would be bedtime, after which this long, long day would finally come to an end.

If only I'd had the courage to switch the set off at nine o'clock. Standing in the pitch darkness now, listening to the dreadful noise they were all making, I knew that for two pins, I'd slip out of the nearest window or door, and run as fast as I could away from Stapley Manor and these horrible children who seemed to be intent on taking my emotions to pieces. Any moment now, I thought, someone like George Ashton will come crashing in again and complete my humiliation.

Suddenly the light came on. I blinked painfully in the direction of the light switch at the other end of the room. It wasn't George Ashton. It was Arnold Ducker.

"Did you want the light on, sir?"

His voice sounded very loud in the hush that had just descended.

"Yes, Arnold," I said, desperately trying to sound as if I was in control of the situation, "Thank you. I was just about to turn it on myself. Right, straighten the chairs and off to bed, everybody."

They all groaned. Colin withdrew a detached chair spring from the small fat boy's nostril, Dennis emerged from behind the television set where he must have hidden when the light went off, and the rest restored the room to a very rough semblance of order. I followed the last boy from the room with a sense of foreboding which turned out to be fully justified. It took me three-quarters of an hour to settle the boys for the night. The quiet reading and drawing of the night before just didn't happen except in the case of a very small number. Most of them seemed to see bedtime as an opportunity to engage in a frantically energetic game of hide-and-seek, in which they hid and I wasn't able to find them. By ten-thirty I felt wrung out. They were all in bed now (as far as I knew) and reasonably quiet. As I dragged my feet along the lower corridor towards the haven of my flat, I was conscious of anger and resentment burning side by side in my heart. How could these boys be so cruelly uncooperative with someone who only wanted to be friendly and helpful? I didn't know how to face the pathetic inept creature that I had been revealed to be over the last fifteen hours. I was useless, and they didn't care.

"Sir."

The loud whisper come from the second room along from my flat—Dennis' room. I stopped and, resting my hands on the door frame, leaned into the room.

"What is it, Dennis? I'm very tired. . ."

Dennis beckoned me to the side of his bed. I levered my weight back to the vertical and took a few steps towards him. All I wanted was to get back to my flat.

"Yes, Dennis. What is it?"

Dennis looked very small in his bed.

"I'm glad you came, sir."

I nearly broke down and cried. Someone had said something nice to me. There was a lump in my throat.

"I'm glad I came too, Dennis." Was that true?

"Mr. Boon used to call me Dennis the Dunce, sir. He made me stand on a chair at mealtimes some days and asked me questions I didn't know. You won't make me do that, will you, sir?"

"No, Dennis. I'll never do that—I promise."

"Thanks, sir. I'm glad you're our housefather."

Dennis turned over sighing contentedly, and was probably sound asleep before I even got out of the room.

Chapter Seven

"Why don't you concentrate on young Dennis for a while? Keep a log for a week or two then come back and discuss it here. I would be extremely interested to hear your observations and comments."

It was the next day and at last I was having my 'chat' with the headmaster, whom I'd hardly seen since starting work. I had woken up that morning with a feeling of overwhelming dread filling my universe. I had to go out and face that mob again. Fortunately, Mark was working as well, so at least I knew that nothing could go drastically wrong. Interestingly, the boys were not as well behaved as they had been on that first morning. They were a little louder, a little less co-operative. I mentioned this to Mark.

"Yes," he said amiably, "good sign really. They're reacting to you as well as me this time."

He tapped me gently on the chest and winked.

"They've noticed you, mate!"

Throughout the morning Mark encouraged me to take a leading role and, secured by the anchor of his presence, I managed to regain a little of the self-respect I'd lost the previous day.

"The thing is," said Mark, as we walked along the bottom corridor after breakfast, "that until you've formed some sort of relationship with the kids, you've got nothing to base anything else on. Doesn't really matter what kind of relationship as long as there is one. Take old Douglas for instance. Sell his grandmother for ten fags. My relationship with him is very simple. He knows that if he crosses me I'll murder him. Simple as that. Now old Colin, he's just a naughty doggy. Pat his head a bit - teach him a few manners, a friend for life. Each one's different, Dave. Don't worry, as soon as they've worked out that you're not Ted Boon, and you're not like Ted Boon, you'll be fine.''

Just then, the boy with the pudding-basin haircut appeared beside us, flushed with hard work.

''Mr. Harper, can you come and check the yard for us please? We've really done it perfect today!''

''There y'go!'' grinned Mark, ''He's not interested in what I think of his blessed yard. Wants Mr. Harper to check it. Great!''

I left the school block after assembly that morning feeling more optimistic than I could possibly have imagined when I'd crawled miserably to bed the night before. If it hadn't been for Dennis' words to me before he went to sleep, I seriously think I might have packed my bags there and then, and left before anyone else got up. Mark's warmth, and his belief that things could change for the better, was very encouraging. Why couldn't George Ashton be like that? He just made me feel useless. . .

''Mr. Harper!''

I had almost reached the Old House entrance when Mrs. Philips called me from the other end of the yard. I walked across, pleased to see her neat, attractive figure again. She smiled brightly at me.

''Mr. Rowley has asked me to see if you could spare him half an hour or so, Mr. Harper. Just for a general chat about things. If you're too busy. . .''

Too busy? Anything was preferable to another lengthy battle with a set of hostile hinges!

''No, Mrs. Philips, that's fine. Do you want me to come over now, or in a minute?''

''Walk over with me,'' said the secretary comfortably. ''How are things going? Are you settling in nicely?''

Mrs. Philips was the sort of person with whom it was very difficult to be anything but positive. I answered with a sort of frenetic lightness.

''Oh, yes, I think it's all going to be fine. One or two little problems, you know, but generally speaking everything's. . . well, fine.''

We entered the office block and stopped outside the door of A.E. Rowley's office, the room where my interview had been held. Mrs. Philips knocked and waited until a voice said something I couldn't hear, then pushed the door open and ushered me in with another sparkling smile of encouragement before closing it again behind me.

A.E. Rowley was sitting behind his desk cleaning a pistol. He looked up, acknowledging my presence with a smiling nod, and a vague gesture towards the armchair beside me. I sat down, semi-hypnotised, unable to take my eyes off the small weapon that the headmaster was polishing so busily with a piece of rag. It was one of those situations where the conversational options seem to be limited to one only.

"Errr. . . I hope you don't mind me asking, Mr. Rowley, but why errr. . .?"

The headmaster's expression was one of polite enquiry.

"Yes, Mr. Harper?"

"I was just wondering why—why you'd got a gun."

He suspended his cleaning operations and looked blankly for a moment at the object in his hand.

"Oh, my pistol you mean."

He lifted it up and swivelled it slightly in his hand so that the light from the window was reflected brightly in the silvery plating.

"My pistol, Mr. Harper, is for use when all else fails."

I was stunned.

"Do you mean suicide or—or self-defence?" I faltered.

Mr. Rowley drew his head back, frowning with perplexity, then suddenly released one of his loud guffaws.

"I do apologise for my lack of clarity, Mr. Harper. No, I have no intention of ending it all at this juncture, nor has it yet become necessary to shoot one of the boys as a warning to the others. Why, I could be severely censured for such an extreme action."

He passed the pistol across to me. I took it gingerly.

"It is in fact a starting pistol" he went on. "It fires blank bullets. Very, very occasionally I fire it towards the ceiling when a conversation or encounter with a child has reached the point where he and I are trapped in one of those dreary, unproductive little playlets that human beings are so prone to indulge in when they have no real wish to communicate. One good bang does much to explode us back into reality.''

The headmaster nodded reflectively to himself, obviously convinced that his explanation of the gun's function was so commonplace and reasonable that no more need be said on the subject. He leaned forward, resting his arms on the desk and studied me for a few moments, his eyes moving slightly from side to side as if he was reading a message on my face.

''Well now, Mr. Harper. . .''

''Please call me David,'' I interrupted.

''Mmmm. . . thank you, but I think that for now I would prefer to address you in a more formal manner. Perhaps, later, when I actually meet David Harper. . .''

I wasn't offended. Why wasn't I offended?

''As I was about to say, Mr. Harper, I asked you to join me this morning for two reasons. First, I should very much like to hear your own assessment of your progress so far, and secondly I am happy to deal with any queries that might have arisen since our last conversation. Please speak freely.''

To my amazement, Mr. Rowley stood up, moved round his desk, and lowered his dignified form to the carpet where he lay on his back with his hands by his sides, quite motionless as I started to speak. I almost forgot he was there after a while. I was lost in the account of my own doings over the last couple of days. For some reason I was able to be totally honest. There is something very vulnerable and unthreatening about someone who is lying corpse-like at your feet. Also, I wanted him to meet David Harper.

''. . . and here I am now,'' I concluded, wondering what the headmaster's reaction would be to my long, rather emotionally charged narrative.

For what seemed a long time he said nothing, just lay still with his eyes closed. It struck me that he might have fallen asleep. I didn't fancy starting the whole thing over again from the beginning when he woke up. He opened his eyes eventually and, with unexpected briskness, pushed himself off the floor and back into a standing position, then sat on the edge of the desk tapping his heels softly against the wooden panelling. Making a vain attempt to smooth his unruly patches of hair with one hand, he gazed musingly through the window, a funny little smile twitching on his lips. He spoke without looking at me.

"For what it's worth, David. . ."

David! I was quite ridiculously thrilled.

"For what it's worth, my first two days in residential childcare were very, very similar to yours. Very similar. I too suffered blistering attacks on my dignity from just such a disembodied, unidentifiable voice as the one which you describe. Perhaps. . ." His voice took on a whimsical note. "Perhaps yours is the same child, frozen at the age of fourteen, doomed by some irresistible force to roam from residential establishment to residential establishment, hurling abuse at new members of staff from obscure corners.. .."

He turned to face me, chuckling as he realised that I was trying to decide whether to laugh obligingly or nod solemnly.

"However," he went on, "there is no doubt about the solid normality of the group as a whole and I can assure you that your experiences so far are predictable and even necessary."

He looked very serious suddenly.

"There are two great dangers for the new residential worker, David. The first is the temptation to model yourself on some other worker, often the first one you work with. Fatal! Equally fatal whether your model is competent or not. Your task is to become the best possible you in your dealings with the children. I know folk who have been in the work for years and years who will never be more than professionally arthritic versions of the first half-reasonable colleague they encountered."

"And the second danger?"

"The second danger is one that your predecessor Mr. Boon did not succeed in avoiding."

I secretly and guiltily looked forward to hearing something juicily negative about the 'wonderful' Mr. Boon.

"Mr. Boon's philosophy of childcare," went on the headmaster, "was, broadly speaking, a rationalisation of his deficiencies, rather than an organically developed method of working."

If Mr. Rowley's words had been pillows, I would have been smothered. I tried to look as if I'd only just misunderstood.

82

"I'm sorry, I don't quite see what you mean. . ."

"He said 'shouldn't' where he should have said 'can't'. He said 'I think this boy shouldn't be forced to do anything he doesn't want to,' where he should have said 'I can't make this boy do anything he doesn't want to.'"

Mr. Rowley continued with some passion.

"He would say that a boy was emotionally frozen when all he meant was that he had been unable to make any kind of relationship with him. He would establish order by making life easier for the larger, more aggressive boys and scaring or ridiculing the younger children such as little Dennis. . ."

He paused for a moment.

"You must find it a little strange that I should criticise your forerunner in this fashion, especially as I was a party to his appointment. But staff are difficult to find and mistakes are made. Mr. Boon did some good—sometimes—for some children, but I do sincerely believe, David, that despite what you described earlier as a disastrous start, you will find your feet and become a very much more sensitive and useful member of staff. You will learn many techniques, and now and then you will be inspired."

He leaned forward and tapped me on the knee.

"I promise you that the business of getting boys to wash is not the primary reason for your presence here. Routine is very important, but it is simply a framework within which we can choose to be flexible if we wish. Once you have relaxed and begun to establish a reasonable day-to-day pattern with the boys, you will find that there are other, more subtle and complex tasks for you to perform. In the meantime. . ."

Whatever the headmaster had been about to say was cut short by Mrs. Philips opening the door without knocking and speaking with some urgency.

"Headmaster, I think you ought to know that Mr. Merry is on his way across the yard with young Howard. I think Howard is having one of his little errr . . . tizzies!"

"Very well, Mrs. Philips," said Mr. Rowley imperturbably, "if you would be so good as to direct them into my office."

I stood up and handed the pistol back to its owner. He placed it in a small drawer in the desk then arranged a piece of paper and a pen in a position to suggest he was in the middle of writing something. I moved towards the door.

"I'll just go and. . ."

"No, no, David, please stay. Howard is a New House boy. Very reasonable and pleasant normally, but subject to occasional violent temper outbursts. Once his temper is defused all will be well."

He sat at his desk, picked up the pen, and appeared to be immediately and totally absorbed in something that he started to write on the sheet of paper.

A series of grunts and crashes and curses suggested that Mike Merry and Howard had arrived outside the office block front door. I backed towards the wall apprehensively. Mr. Rowley continued to write with apparent unconcern. A few seconds later the mobile pitched battle arrived at the door of the office and finally came into view for the first time. I had always believed that those Beano-type cartoon fights, where all that can be seen is a cloud of dust with arms and legs sticking out, were amusing but gross exaggerations, but that was how the scene in front of me appeared. As far as I could make out, Mike Merry was simply attempting to restrain Howard. It was Howard's frantic determination not to be restrained that was causing all the commotion. Every time the big, bearded man secured a grip on a wrist, a foot would detach itself and aim a hard kick at whichever part of Mike Merry's anatomy was available. Mike would then grab the ankle attached to the offending foot and lose his hold on the wrist, which was of course connected to a fist. The fist would then thump Mike as hard as possible—and so on. The boy was not large but he looked very tough and slippery. He had the added advantage that he obviously didn't care how much damage he inflicted on his adversary whereas Mike Merry, whose good nature shone through all his cussing and crossness with the boy, was clearly working hard to avoid causing Howard any pain. The boy's language was pungent and versatile. I looked at the headmaster. He was still writing quietly. To all appearances he was quite oblivious of the mini-war being fought out on the carpet in front of him. After a few seconds he stood up, still holding the sheet of paper in his hand, and moved round the desk towards the battling pair. On reaching them he bent from the waist until his face was next to the purple, tear-streaked face of the struggling boy. He spoke into the melee with the utmost politeness.

"Howard, old chap," he said apologetically, "I'm awfully sorry to interrupt. I can see you're busy, but. . ." He tapped his sheet of paper with one finger. "I can't quite remember how you spell you surname. Would you mind just. . . ?"

There was a lull in the conflict as Howard's attention was wrenched away from Mike Merry by the sheer incongruity of Mr. Rowley's manner and question. He sniffed, and spoke in a trembly voice.

"It's errr. . . spelt like b-b-bridge with an 'r' on the end, sir. B-r-i-d-g-e-r."

The headmaster leaned the piece of paper on his knee and wrote carefully.

"Thank you, Howard. Thank you very much indeed."

He stood up and went back to his desk.

"Errr. . . carry on, Howard," he added, settling back into his chair and bending over the desktop.

Howard, hanging limply by an ankle and a hand, became aware suddenly that he was no longer fighting. He started to struggle again, not as fiercely as before, but still with considerable vigour. Mr. Rowley called out from his desk.

"Howard! Look, I really am terribly sorry, but I need to check your address as well. Could you come over here just for a moment—please. If you could put Howard down, Mr. Merry? Thank you."

Finding himself deposited on the floor, Howard stood up and quite docilely joined the headmaster behind the desk. After a prolonged discussion about the details of the boy's home address, A.E. Rowley suddenly looked hard at Howard as though he'd remembered something rather less important.

"Howard," he said, "I meant to ask you, were you having a disagreement with Mr. Merry just now?"

Howard, a stocky little boy with curly dark hair and a miniature prize-fighter's features, smiled sheepishly. All the tension and aggression had apparently disappeared.

"Yes, sir," he said in a hoarse, throaty voice. "It wuz all my fault though. I got inter a bit of a tizz 'coz I couldn't get my blinkin' work right."

He flashed a smile of quite exceptional brilliance across at Mike Merry, who was busily rubbing his shin.

"Sorry, Mike," he said. "'Ope I didn't 'urt yer. I'm an idiot aren't I?"

The teacher grinned back at him warmly. He seemed to forgive him on the spot. He spoke with a strong west country accent.

"Alright, Twinkle. I'll get you back somehow. Come on, let's get into school and have a look at that work of yours."

Teacher and boy left the room side by side, the big man's arm resting on Howard's shoulders. They seemed the best of friends. I decided I ought to get to know Mike Merry. He looked a very likeable man. I turned to Mr. Rowley

"Why did he call him Twinkle?"

The headmaster leaned back in his chair, his pen clenched between his teeth like a cigar.

"We nicknamed him Twinkle," he replied, "because of that smile. Marvellous is it not? He is also a boy with a powerful sense of justice. When you leave here in a moment it will be break time and I am quite certain that you will discover Howard furiously engaged in some kind of hard physical work such as digging. It will be an entirely voluntary way of paying for the temper outburst that you saw just now. Eventually we hope to do something about these episodes, but until Howard gains more confidence and belief in himself, distraction is our most useful weapon."

He leaned forward and placed the biro back on the desk.

"Anyway, as I was about to say when Mrs. Philips came in, I would like to suggest that you make a close study of one of the boys in your house. I think that would be a useful activity."

Mr. Rowley's suggestion that I should concentrate on Dennis was a very welcome one. I already had a soft spot for the timid little boy. I looked forward to finding out what really went on inside him.

"The other thing I wanted to say to you," said the headmaster after we had talked about Dennis, "was that I do sincerely hope you develop your friendship with Tom. Very often the staff from one house can be very useful to boys from the other, not least because your role is able to be a non-controlling one. And in any case, I feel that you in particular will be able to establish a real bond with Tom. So. . ?"

"Yes," I promised. "Yes, of course. I'll do my best. I suppose," I added nervously, "that the housefather in the New House won't mind if I. . ."

Mr. Rowley's face became a wooden mask.

"Mr. Hepton does not have the option of non-cooperation," he said, with such finality that I didn't dare to say any more on the subject. He looked at his watch.

"Did you wish to ask me anything, David? I'm afraid time is. . ."

"Well," I replied, "I was going to ask you what you thought maladjustment really was, but I realise you have to get on."

After a moment's silence, the headmaster jerked his chair round so that he was facing the window again, swung his legs up and plonked his feet down on the desk. Resting his head back on interlinked hands he quoted softly.

Stranded in the hall of mirrors
I can nevermore avoid
Images that cannot show me
Something long ago destroyed.

In the darkness, in the distance
In a corner of my mind
Stands a puzzled child in silence
Lonely, lost, and far behind.

In imagination only
In my single mirror see
Clear and calm, the one reflection
Of the person that is me.

He turned and looked at me.

"We'll go into the more technical definitions when we have time, David. In the meantime, remember that for all the boys at Stapley Manor, and the boys in the Old House particularly, you are one of those mirrors—and an important one."

As I got up and moved towards the door, I wondered if A.E. Rowley realised to what an extent those verses had struck a chord in me. It had been a strange moment. I stopped at the door.

"Mr. Rowley—just now, before Howard errr. . . came in, did you know what you were going to do?"

"Goodness gracious, no!" said the headmaster. "Until I actually walked over to the boy I had not the faintest idea what to do. But—and this is important—I knew I was going to do something!"

The headmaster was quite right about Howard—or Twinkle. The first thing I saw as I left the office block was a small sturdy figure toiling away energetically with a garden fork in one of the flower beds. He looked up as I passed and gave me another of those film star smiles.

"Wotcha, sir," he called cheerily. "Alright?"

Twinkle was one of those people—and it doesn't seem to matter how young or old they are—who flatter you just by noticing you. I waved back.

"Hello, Howard. Yes, I'm fine, thanks!"

As I walked on I wondered what I would do if the 'twinkle' faded when I was around and one of those awful tempers was aimed at me. I hoped I'd never find out.

I wasn't due to work that evening so I intercepted Mike Merry as he was about to climb into his car at the end of the school day and arranged to meet him for a drink later on in one of the Stapley pubs. His name suited him well. He turned out to be very genial company indeed. He was quite happy to describe horrendous incidents that had occurred in his own brief career as a teacher of maladjusted boys. He'd been at Stapley Manor for a year now, he told me, and he was just beginning to really enjoy it.

"Mind you," he chuckled, wiping beer froth from his beard contentedly, "I'm still not very good at controlling the little beggars. I don't mind too much though. They're good kids really, and I've got Jean and my two little girls to go home to at the end of the day."

How cosy, I thought, as I licked the end of my finger and dipped it into the pile of roast peanut dust in front of me. That's what I need—someone to come home to, someone like Annie. . .

"Now old Rowley," went on Mike, "I dunno. . . he's a blinking magician, that's what he is. Look at today with Twinkle. A blinking magician! I don't know how he thinks of these things."

He gazed into his glass for a moment.

"Helped me a lot actually. Good bloke, the Head. Believes in you, if you know what I mean."

"What about the other housefather," I asked, "what's he like? I haven't met him yet. Hepton isn't it?"

"Yeah, that's right. Steve Hepton. He's on holiday at the moment. He'll be back at the weekend. He's okay. Another pint?"

For some reason Mike obviously didn't want to talk about my New House counterpart. I changed the subject and told him about my commission from Mr. Rowley to study Dennis. He seemed pleased.

"I like the idea of someone taking special notice of little Den," he said. "The kid's had a bit of a rough time in some ways."

He peered thoughtfully into the distance for a second or two.

"Tell you what, Dave. There's something I've noticed about old Den. Might be something for you to follow up if you're interested. It's a bit of a mystery really—mystery to me anyway."

He leaned forward, his brows wrinkled in concentration.

"You see, every now and then, I've had to do a morning in the Old House, even though I usually do my extraneous duties on the other side, and a right pig's ear I've made of it most times. But in between wrestling with Martin and whatever, I've spotted something, and it's the same every single time. You see. . ."

I waited while half a pint disappeared down the big man's throat. He placed his empty glass down and went on.

"Dennis always does his job, always makes his bed and all that, and he's always there in the line when assembly time comes - good as gold always. But every morning, when he's had his job and his room checked, he just seems to disappear for, ooh. . . about ten minutes. It took me a few times to see it was happening because I was so busy with the rest of the bloomin' circus, but after a few times I was sure. I asked Ted Boon once - the bloke before you—where Den went every morning, but he said he hadn't even noticed it. So. . . there's the mystery, Dave. Where does he go? You find that out and I'd be really interested to know the answer. He doesn't smoke, so it can't be that. He wouldn't dare do anything wrong. What's going on? Interesting, eh?"

It was interesting. As I climbed back up the hill later that night, I felt quite excited. I would ferret out the secret of Dennis' morning trips all on my own and that would be the first major item to go down in my log. Back to my flat, I sat down to write an account of the last two days to Annie. I made it as detailed and dramatic as possible. I wanted her to feel what I'd felt—good or bad, up or down. Dear Annie. How I missed her. I thought of Mike Merry going home to his family. Someone to talk to—to be with. As I sat at the little table in my sitting room, I felt desperately lonely suddenly. I'd never been very good at being on my own, despite my tendency to retreat. So difficult to know who I really was when nobody else was there: "In imagination only. . ."

I finished the letter with a description of the Great Dennis Mystery. That cheered me up. When I saw Annie next week I'd be able to reveal the solution. I sealed and stamped the envelope ready to post in the morning. I must have sat by my window staring out into the darkness for ages before going to bed that night.

The next morning, working on my own, I had little chance to investigate Dennis' secret. I did notice that he was not around for a time, but I was far too occupied to look for him, even if I'd known where to start. It was a better day than the first one I spent alone, but there were still many battles and frustrations, Colin in particular going out of his way to take offence at a number of things I did and said throughout the day, subtly prodded, I guessed, by Douglas, who was still pursuing a policy of strategic politeness as far as I was concerned.

On Friday, though, I had my chance. Over an early cup of tea with Mark Parish, I described what Mike had said and what I wanted to do. He was fascinated.

"The little beggar!" he chuckled delightedly. "You know, Mike's dead right now I think about it. I've often noticed that we're short by one whole Dennis for a while in the morning. Not that it's worried me. In fact. . . "

He shifted his weight in my armchair as a fresh thought struck him.

"A few times he's actually come and asked me if he could go for a little walk before school starts. Never occurred to me to wonder why, it being Dennis, you know. So you want to do a Sherlock Holmes on him this morning do you, Dave?''

"Well, yes, if that's alright, Mark. I'd just like to follow him and see where he pops off to.''

Mark spread his hand widely.

"I'm just a humble pedagogue, Dave. Over here you're the boss. Tell me what to do and I'll just follow orders.''

He winked broadly.

"Just so long as you tell me all about it afterwards!''

Later that morning, when breakfast was over and I was checking sullen Martin's shower block job, I heard Mark calling me from the ground floor. I arrived at the foot of the stairs to find Mark calmly filling his pipe and Dennis hopping nervously from foot to foot beside him.

"Ah, Mr. Harper,'' said Mark gravely. "Young Dennis here has asked if he can go for a 'little walk' before assembly. What do you think? Reckon he should go?''

"Yes,'' I said, nodding judiciously, "Yes, I think that would be alright.''

"Thank you, sir!'' said the anxious little boy. He turned and scuttled quickly out of the door into the yard.

I leaned my head out of the doorway. Dennis, in his usual strange manner, was making his way towards the line of poplars at the edge of the grounds. I glanced back and nodded at Mark, then stepped out and started strolling casually in the same direction as the small erratic figure.

Chapter Eight

"Hello, Eric, are you still my friend? You're lookin' very well, John. Nice morning, eh? Hello, Bob! How's your leaves today?"

I had discovered Dennis' secret. He was talking to trees.

At the end of the Old House building a little track ran off from the gravel path that encircled the house. It led between some thick bushes into a clearing that overlooked Stapley on the left, and the fields sloping down from the sewage plant on the right. Whoever designed the house in the first place must have loved silver birch trees. At the back of the clearing near the bushes was a little stand of birches, six in all, not as large as the ones near Mr. Rowley's house but a very attractive sight in the morning sunshine.

Dennis was standing in the centre of this group of trees, chattering animatedly. From a convenient point near the bushes I could hear most of what he was saying. Each tree seemed to have a name and a definite personality. From the way Dennis spoke to them it was clear that he was absolutely indispensable as friend and advisor to his tall, slim friends. As he spoke he left little pauses, during which, presumably, they spoke to him.

"How are you, Michael? Have you been thinkin' 'bout what I said?"

Pause.

"You have been thinkin' 'bout what I said! Good tree! You got some more water in your roots like I said, did you? Good! So I was right, wasn't I?"

Pause.

"You want to be my what, Michael?"

A breeze ruffled the leaves in the tops of the trees. Dennis glanced round sternly.

"Sssh, everybody," he admonished, "Michael's tryin' to say somethin' to me."

Pause.

"You want to be my special friend, Michael? Well, I dunno. . ."

Dennis sighed like one who is oppressed with the constant demands imposed by popularity.

"I gotta be friends with all of you," he explained. His eyes brightened. "Tell you what! I'll be special friends to all of you! Every single one!"

This clearly resulted in a chorus of grateful thanks from the arboreal assembly, as Dennis made a little circuit of the copse, executing small deprecating movements with one hand, and patting trunks indulgently with the other. There was no doubt that, whatever Dennis might be anywhere else, here he was a hero and a star. He addressed them all once more.

"Well, gotta go I'm 'fraid. They need me in school now. See you tomorrow, all my friends."

Dennis hugged the tree nearest to him then moved to the next. He was going to hug them all, just like he'd hugged the big fir tree when I first met him. I slipped back down the path between the bushes and round to the yard. By the time Dennis appeared round the corner of the building I was leaning against the wall, watching the pudding basin boy, whose name I had learned was Henry, put some hurried finishing touches to his yard job.

"Okay, Dennis?" I called, as the small figure flapped towards me. "Had a nice walk?"

He twitched to a halt beside me.

"Yes thanks, sir."

I thought again how much Dennis reminded me of Piglet. Obviously he badly needed a Pooh Bear.

"Dennis—may I ask you a question?"

The boy's eagerness to cooperate was so great that it seemed to block his efforts to answer. His body quivered with goodwill.

"Yes, sir!" he managed at last. "Ask me a sum—I like sums!"

"Err. . . no, I didn't mean that sort of question," I said, disconcerted for a moment. "I want to ask you something else, Dennis. Have you got a friend here at school, a real friend I mean?"

He looked at the ground, suddenly still.

"'Aven't got one, sir."

"What about Arnold Ducker? He sits on your table, doesn't he? Are you not friendly with him?"

Dennis still didn't look up. He stirred a loose piece of tarmac with his foot.

"Arnold's clever, sir. He's gonna get Whole levels an' Hay levels. I don't understand him when 'e starts."

He looked up suddenly, his eyes shining.

"I have got a friend though, sir. He's called Brian. He writes to me. D'you want me to show you the letters, sir? I've got lots."

I was surprised—pleased, but surprised. It seemed odd that Dennis should have a regular correspondent. I noticed that the other boys were lining up by the steps. Henry had dashed off to put his brush away.

"Could I have a look at them this evening after tea, Dennis? I'd love to see them all then."

"Yes, sir!" said the boy excitedly. "After tea, sir!"

He dashed off to join the others.

Half an hour later, as I pretended to repair the same things that I had failed to get anywhere with all week, I realised that there was bound to be some sort of showdown with George Ashton before long. He was hardly looking at me now, let alone talking to me. It was only a matter of time before he woke up to the fact that I was to DIY what Herod was to mothercare. Toiling hopelessly with viciously uncooperative screws, and wood that split with a sneer every time I thought I'd scored a minor success, I wished I had been more honest at the interview. Returning my armful of tools to the woodwork room at half past ten, I glanced round at the handful of boys bent busily over fruit bowls and towel racks and elementary aeroplane shapes. George Ashton was over in the far corner working on the lathe. I'd been told he was very good with children, but I didn't know what form these so-called skills might take. Perhaps I'd find out soon.

I hurried back to my flat, anxious to begin the first entry in my 'Dennis log'. It was satisfying to have solved the problem so quickly and I was looking forward to adding some details about the mysterious 'Brian' after my chat with Dennis this evening.

As it turned out, I wasn't able to look at Dennis' letters until much later in the evening, and by then I had gathered a lot more unexpected material for my log.

Friday, I discovered, was a very significant day at Stapley Manor. After school had finished, the boys divided into two separate but equally tense groups. One group was made up of those who were going home for the weekend. They displayed a rich mixture of anxiety and excitement as they prepared for their two-day excursion into situations that, by definition, they were not adjusted to. Ruth Crompton was on hand to help this group with their packing and general preparations. She was also a marvellously calming influence on boys who were particularly nervous. Robert, for instance, was so concerned that he might spoil his "clean and smart" image, that he stood stiffly in the very centre of the yard next to his suitcase from the moment he was ready until the moment he was allowed to climb into the school van at five o'clock. Occasionally he glanced fearfully from side to side as though afraid that some item of uncleanness might be wafted on to him by the breeze. Ruth told me that Robert's mother always investigated every item of clothing in her son's suitcase minutely to check that it was perfectly clean and well-preserved. A single flaw could destroy the entire weekend for Robert.

Cars came and went throughout the period between school and teatime, as parents picked their children up and drove them away. I was vaguely surprised to note that the mothers and fathers looked like perfectly normal human beings. I'm not sure what I expected—some separate monstrous breed I suppose. I noted that Ruth seemed to be on very easy, friendly speaking terms with most of them. By a quarter to five there were only the van boys left. These were the ones who would be driven down to the bus station, or home if they lived locally. By five o'clock they too were gone and I was left with the handful of boys who made up the second kind of group.

These were the boys who, for one reason or another, would not be going home for the weekend. They too seemed to be experiencing a mixture of emotions. In their case it was a combination of sadness and relief. They would like to have gone home but were only too well aware of the problems that could arise once they got there. Arnold Ducker, who was standing beside me as I watched the van disappear round the office block, put it rather well.

"If the whole weekend was made up of first five minuteses, sir, it would be great, but it's not."

Personally, I experienced a great lifting of spirits as boy after boy departed. What a luxury it would be to have only five boys to deal with this evening. I could really relax and get to know one or two of them, especially as the more difficult ones were out of the way until Sunday evening. At five o'clock I sat down for tea with four of the remaining group. One missing. I knew there should be five because Ruth had shown me the list. I looked at those present. Arnold Ducker and Anthony, the fat boy, on my table. Henry and his yard-sweeping colleague, James, on the other.

"Who's missing?" I asked Arnold, who seemed to know most things.

He looked surprised.

"Dennis of course, sir. He sits on our table, doesn't he?"

How extraordinary! How could I possibly have forgotten Dennis of all people? I stood up.

"Carry on quietly with your tea, everybody. I'm just going to look for Dennis. Don't eat my tea, Anthony. I'll be back for it in a minute."

"He'll be in his room looking out of the window, sir," said Arnold mechanically, "because of it being Friday."

Restraining myself from questioning this strange piece of reasoning, I hurried through the games room, up the back stairs and along the corridor to Dennis' room. Arnold was quite right. Dennis was leaning on his windowsill, gazing out through the open window in the direction of the lane that climbed up from Stapley. There was a suitcase standing on the floor beside him, and he seemed to be more smartly dressed than usual. I stopped at the door.

"Dennis—tea's already started. What are you doing?"

Dennis glanced round briefly.

"Waitin' for my dad, sir. He's a bit late. I'm watchin' out for our car comin' up the lane. It's a big blue one, sir."

Confused, I joined Dennis at the window. The view was exactly the same as the one from my flat. It was very grey now over the hills. Rain on the way.

"Dennis," I said, "I don't understand. You're not down for. . ."

Ruth Crompton, breathless and tense looking, appeared suddenly in the doorway and interrupted me.

"Mr. Harper! Err. . . I forgot to mention to you earlier that Dennis' dad would probably be coming to pick him up just before teatime. I'm so sorry. My fault entirely."

"But he wasn't. . ."

Ruth broke in again, speaking to Dennis this time.

"Dennis, love. It looks as if your dad hasn't been able to make it this week. I expect something's gone wrong and he's ever so disappointed not to be able to take you home for the weekend. I expect that's what's happened, don't you?"

"Yes, miss," said Dennis. "I expect the car's gone wrong again, miss."

He threw one more wistful look towards the lane, then turned and looked up at Ruth again.

"Shall I unpack an' go down to tea then, miss?"

"I tell you what," said Ruth kindly, planting her hands firmly on his shoulders, "you go down and have your tea and I'll unpack for you. Okay?"

"Yes, miss," said Dennis gratefully, smiling up at her.

She patted his shoulders twice.

"Off you go!"

I was about to follow him but Ruth laid a hand on my arm.

"Hold on a tick, David," she said quietly.

She picked up Dennis' suitcase from the floor and laid it on one of beds, then turned to me again.

"We go through this ritual just about every Friday."

"You mean. . .?"

"Dennis' father has arrived once to take him home for a weekend in all the time he's been here, but Dennis has to go on playing this little game of expecting him every Friday or everything falls apart for him."

"You said he's playing a game," I protested, "but he didn't look as if he was playing a game. He looked as if he really believed it."

Ruth didn't answer. She sat on the bed, turned the suitcase towards her and, flicking the catches, pushed the lid back. The suitcase was empty.

That first Friday evening at Stapley Manor was quite delightful. I organised a snooker tournament with my five charges and sent Henry down to the village to buy some sweets to use as prizes. Henry's friend James, a solidly built, very pleasantly placid boy, won the first prize easily, but I had made sure there were second, third, fourth and fifth prizes as well. Dennis, who normally didn't get much of a look in on the snooker table, enjoyed himself enormously, despite the fact that his almost total lack of co-ordination meant that he failed to pot anything except the white cue ball. Each time, regardless of the fact that this automatically incurred a penalty of at least four points, he would throw his arms in the air exultantly and shout "I got one, sir!"

By the time the group settled down in the TV room to watch a final programme before bedtime, I was feeling more mellow than at any time since the beginning of the week. Supper had been a quiet, civilised affair involving many 'pleases' and 'thank-yous', quite different from the ill-mannered riot that happened when I was on my own with the whole group. I sensed that the little band who had been left for the weekend were quietly relishing the special familial feel of the evening. At least—four of them were. Anthony, the fat boy, seemed to relish only one thing and that was the consumption of foodstuffs. He ate whatever he could get, whenever he could get it, and I had yet to see him show any interest in anything else. He had been the only one not to take his plate and mug into the kitchen after supper without being told. The others had rounded on him, clearly annoyed that he should do anything to disrupt the gently glowing atmosphere of the occasion. But I sensed that Anthony was not sensitive to atmospheres. You couldn't eat atmospheres. His little eyes had glinted with anger as he gave in to pressure and carried his things out. I got the feeling that when Anthony was angry he would make sure that, when it could be done secretly, someone somewhere would suffer.

Bedtime that night was a joy. There they were, just as they had been when Mark was on, sitting up in bed occupied quietly with harmless activities. I chatted a little to each boy, leaving Dennis until last. Arnold Ducker was studying an atlas when I came into his room. He looked up.

"It's better when there's only a few, isn't it, sir?" he said.

"Yes, Arnold. It's completely different. I've really enjoyed this evening."

"They'll all be back on Sunday though, sir, won't they? I don't like it when they come back, sir. They have to take it out on somebody."

"Take what out, Arnold? What do you mean?"

"Home and that, sir. They get all upset and take it out on somebody when they come back."

I was getting used to Arnold being a greater expert on his environment than I was.

"Yes," I replied, "I'm sure you're right. Very understandable, of course. Anyway, goodnight, Arnold."

As I turned away from the bed, Arnold, who had laid his atlas down on his locker and was snuggling down under the blankets, called me back.

"Mr. Harper."

"Yes, Arnold?"

"Will you tuck me in please, sir?"

"Errr. . . yes, of course, Arnold."

I moved round the bed, tucking in sheets and blankets tightly as I went.

"Okay, Arnold?" I asked, as I finished and stood up straight again.

Arnold spoke once more in his resonant, oddly emotionless voice.

"I asked Mr. Boon to tuck me in once, sir, when I first came, but he said I was a poof, sir. But I'm not."

"I know you're not, Arnold," I said quietly. "Goodnight."

Dennis was obviously straining his jug-like ears to the utmost as he awaited my visit. Before I even reached the door of his room he called out.

"I've gottem, sir! They're here! I've gottem!"

Spread out on the bed in front of him were several sheets of paper, each one a brief, badly spelt note from his friend Brian, whose name was signed in a large, untidy scrawl. I picked one up and read it.

> dir Dennis,
> how ar you i am well
> how ar you see you soon
> yor frend
> luv brian

The other notes were very similar. There was neither date nor address on any of them. Still, they were letters from a friend and that was all that mattered to Dennis. I decided to copy one into my log.

"Would you mind if I borrowed one for a little while, Dennis, just to . . . well, to look at?"

"Borrow 'em all, sir!" said Dennis expansively, pleased at this extra interest in his friend's communications. "Look at 'em all, sir!"

"Oh, well," I thought as I went back to my flat with the little pile of papers, "I might as well take them all if it makes him happy."

I sat down at my small table and began to record the business of Dennis' non-existent weekend at home. Two or three minutes later there was a tap on the door and Ruth Crompton came in.

"Hello, David," she said, "I've got some news that might interest you . . . hello! What are these?"

Her eye had spotted the heap of papers on the table by my notebook. She picked the top one up and read it, then put it back with a puzzled expression on her face.

"They're letters from Dennis' friend Brian," I explained. "I'm just going to write about them in my 'Dennis file'. It's great that he's got a friend like that, especially after what I saw earlier today."

I described what I had witnessed after following Dennis that morning. When I'd finished Ruth nodded gently, visibly moved. She picked up the letter again.

"I see. So this. . ."

"And bearing in mind the business about the weekend as well, it seems especially important to me that Dennis has a real friend like Brian, because all the rest is just fantasy, and that can't be very good for a boy of his age."

I was beginning to rather enjoy the sound of my own voice.

"I mean, why shouldn't we get Dennis to invite Brian down here for the weekend, or even arrange for Dennis to go and stay with Brian's family for a day or two? It would be a terrific. . ."

Ruth held up an arresting hand.

"David, just before you go on, can I check something? I won't be a moment."

She hurried out, sorting through a big bunch of keys as she went. I laid my pen down, scratched my head and sighed. I wanted to get on with my writing. Five minutes later Ruth was back. There something in her hand. She laid it down on the table.

"Look," she said. "This is Dennis' English book."

She opened the exercise book and placed one of Brian's letters next to a page of writing. I studied them in silence for a few moments.

I felt the blood rushing to my cheeks. All those things I'd said about Brian coming to stay and Dennis staying with Brian! I looked up.

"Yes, Ruth!" I replied. "The handwriting's the same. Dennis wrote those letters himself. How could I have been so stupid?"

"Don't blame yourself, David. I only thought it was a bit odd because I often collect the post in the morning and I couldn't remember ever seeing a single letter addressed to Dennis, let alone all these."

I tapped the pile of papers.

"Shouldn't we do something about these though, Ruth. The boy seems to be living in a total fantasy world. The trees and the weekend and these letters—I dunno. . ."

"Well, that's all very well, David, but what are you going to replace all these things with? He hasn't got a real friend, and

101

as for his father he may have stopped beating Dennis up, but quite frankly he couldn't care less about the boy. Until he's got something real I don't see how we can take away the little that Dennis has got, even if it's only in his imagination."

"Hmmm. . . yes, I suppose you're right."

I wasn't convinced, but I'd only been doing the job for a week. Ruth was an old hand. I smiled ruefully as I picked up the "Brian" letters.

"Okay, Ruth. I'll just pop these back into Dennis' room and leave it at that. Let's hope a real friend comes along for Dennis soon."

The little matron moved towards the door.

"Amen to that, David. Anyway, I'd better let you get to bed—Oh! I still haven't told you what I came up here to tell you. . ."

She looked quite excited.

"The housefather and housemother in the New House are a married couple, the Heptons, be we haven't been able to recruit a housemother for this side since the last one left six months ago. No applicants, wrong applicants—it just didn't work out. So. . . I was wondering. . ."

She paused.

"Yes?" I prompted.

"Well, I was wondering if your Annie might care to apply for the job. Just a thought. . ."

Just a thought. What a thought! I woke up twice that night trying to remember why I felt so excited. Imagine having Annie here with me—working with me. She'd be ideal in so many ways. The boys would think she was wonderful. So would everyone else. It would be. . . well, what a thought!

I phoned Annie the next morning while my little group (all but Dennis) were down in Stapley with their pocket money. I probably got a bit too pushy. Annie's response was guarded.

"It's a very attractive idea, David, but you do realise that we'd be living in each other's pockets all day and every day?"

"I don't mind living in your pocket, Annie," I said as plaintively as possible. "I think it would be great! Just think—all the walks over the hills, going down to the coast at weekends and on days off, being together in the evenings. I can't imagine anything nicer. . ."

"Let me just think about it, David. I'm missing you so much at the moment that I could easily say I'll go ahead and apply without really thinking about it properly. I'm seeing you on Monday. I'll think about it between now and then. Oh, David, I am looking forward to seeing you. . ."

I enjoyed a pleasant cup of coffee with Mike Merry in the New House that morning. We were joined by Mrs. Murchison, the cook, a very friendly northerner, and also, to my surprise, by Tom, who sat sipping his coffee and listening to the conversation just as if he was another member of staff. When I walked back at half past eleven, I found that Tom had followed me through the swing doors into the Old House dining room. Something told me that I would be unwise to be too enthusiastic in my response to this approach. I collected some cutlery from the trays on the hatch and began to lay up two tables ready for lunch. I was aware of the boy's quiet presence by the door. It was as if something new and fragile was forming in the corner where he stood. If I said the wrong thing I could easily smash it. I said nothing. Eventually, Tom spoke.

"Are you working all day tomorrow, sir?"

I straightened a table mat with exaggerated concentration and replied as abstractedly and lightly as possible.

"Not all day, Tom. I'm off until about three o'clock. They all start coming back then, don't they. I think Mr. Parish is on in the morning over here, but I'm not sure."

There was a long silence. I reached the last place-setting. Never has a place been laid with such minute and time consuming care. Finally, I bent low over the table scratching at a non-existent mark on the wooden surface. Tom spoke again.

"I might go for a walk tomorrow, sir."

I looked at him and nodded casually.

"Mmmm, good idea. I went for a walk the other day, Tom. Right over the hills. It was tremendous. Really blew the dust away. I haven't been up the Peak yet though. I'm not absolutely sure how you get at it."

"I could show you tomorrow if you like, sir. It's a little path through the hedge about a hundred yards up the road."

103

"Oh, well," I sounded pleasantly surprised. "If you don't mind, Tom, I'd be grateful. How about half past ten? I'll come and find you."

"Alright," said Tom gravely, "half past ten, sir."

He moved suddenly towards the swing doors and a moment later had disappeared.

The rest of the day was as relaxed as the Friday evening had been. Henry and James unearthed a large car-racing set from the cupboard at the foot of the main stairs, and spent most of the afternoon and evening crawling around the games room floor "fixing" cars and searching for faulty connections in the dusty old track. I don't suppose the two cars were actually running for more than about fifteen minutes in total, but the boys seemed quite content. Arnold and Dennis asked if we could play Cheat again after tea. I tried to prise Anthony away from his desultory perusal of the pile of old comics in the corner of the games room but, having ascertained that there was no food involved, he just shook his head dolefully and went back to his reading.

Arnold's enjoyment of Cheat had increased enormously now that he understood the point of the game. He shamelessly "cheated" at every opportunity, and having an extraordinarily good memory he was frequently able to detect my pathetic attempts to palm off two kings as four aces. Dennis' understanding of the game on the other hand seemed to have decreased. He would shout "CHEAT!" very loudly after playing his own cards, even when he hadn't cheated, which led to some confusion. The game continued until suppertime, when the boys pleaded to be allowed to take their soup and biscuits into the TV room so that they could watch a film from the beginning. As I sauntered easily along the corridor from the TV room towards the kitchen, hoping to find some supper for myself now that the boys were settled, I heard voices coming from the yard, and a moment later Mr. Rowley appeared at the other end of the corridor accompanied by a rather odd-looking child whom I had never seen before.

"Ah, there you are, David. May I introduce. . ."

He patted the boy's head gently.

"This is Desmond."

I looked at Desmond. If ever there was an ill-favoured child it was Desmond. Everything about him had a stunted look, like one of those miniature Japanese trees, but without their carefully cultivated symmetry. One foot turned out, the other turned in. His body seemed to have a list to one side, and his head tilted the opposite way. His face, creased and twisted, looked as if it had shrunk after being put in the wash, and his hair, which shot straight up from the top of his head in a coarse black brush, gave him a permanently surprised expression. In all, he looked as if he had been constructed very badly from a cheap human being kit. At the same time taking in all these visual details, I became aware that there was a very unpleasant odour emanating from his general direction. Assuming that Mr. Rowley was not responsible for it, it had to be coming from Desmond.

"Hello, Desmond," I said.

To my surprise the boy drew himself up as straight as his awkwardly shaped body would allow, clicked his heels together, and saluted in soldierly fashion.

"Sah!" he shouted, as though he had been addressed by an officer on the parade ground.

Inexperienced though I was, I detected a great fear behind this strange presentation. I looked enquiringly at Mr. Rowley.

"Errr. . . just before we discuss the situation," said the headmaster, "is it possible for one of the other boys to come and show Desmond around the house for a few minutes?"

I fetched Dennis, who was more than happy to undertake the responsible task of guiding Desmond through the Old House. They disappeared together round the corner at the end of the corridor. I heard Dennis say, "These are the stairs. . ."

Mr. Rowley looked slightly embarrassed.

"It is very rare, David, that I would consider admitting a boy at very short notice. The procedure is usually fairly lengthy. Referrals to a psychologist, interviews, testing, etc., but just occasionally I am faced with requests that are very difficult to refuse. Desmond has been referred, but the process was incomplete. This morning however, his foster parents finally rejected him totally, and I have been asked to avoid a series of moves for the boy by admitting him immediately, and I have agreed. I hope this will not be an inconvenience for you this evening. If so, I am quite happy to stay and see Desmond in, as it were."

Mr. Rowley probably never realised how much I was built up that evening by the deferential tone of his speech. As time went by I was to learn that the headmaster invariably regarded the person who was actually on duty as being in a very special position.

"Oh no, that's fine, Mr. Rowley—no trouble at all. Errr. . . why did the foster parents reject errr. . . Desmond?"
Mr. Rowley rubbed an ear vigorously and sucked air in loudly through his teeth.

"We-e-ll, his general level of competence is very, very low, and there has been little or no improvement in his basic skills during the time he spent with this couple. But the thing that finally wore them out was his chronic encupresis."

"N-q-what?"

"I'm sorry, David. There's no reason why you should be familiar with the term. It means that Desmond has problems in controlling his bowel movements. He regularly soils his pants and occasionally his bed. Ruth will come in tomorrow to help Desmond to establish a routine for keeping himself clean, but in the meantime he will need a plastic bucket filled with water and disinfectant. He will need that very soon."

I nodded.

"You mean that smell was. . .?"

"Quite," said the headmaster. "He was very frightened and nervous on arrival. The result was totally predictable. If I may say so, David, I would, if I were you, speak to Desmond about his soiling as if it was a familiar and quite undisgusting phenomenon. I appreciate that this is quite new to you but it really might be best to approach it in that manner. In the meantime. . .?"

"Yes?"

"Who on earth can he share a room with? It would hardly be fair. . ."

At that moment, Dennis and Desmond, after what must have been a very brisk tour of the two upper corridors, reappeared at the bottom of the back stairs, laughing together as they made their ricketty way towards us. The smell was worse.

"Please, sir," said Dennis imploringly, "Can Desmond be in my room, sir? We're friends! We're gonna be friends!"

"Private Dennis and I would like to share a room," said Desmond in his slow creaky voice.

I looked at Mr. Rowley, who then looked at Desmond.

106

"Private Desmond," he said, "may I tell Private Dennis about your problem?"

Desmond nodded, suddenly drawn and anxious.

"Dennis, you ought to know that Desmond messes himself quite often. It smells bad. Do you mind sharing your room with Desmond even though he does that? He does need a friend who will help him by not telling everybody else about his problem and go around with him—that sort of thing. What do you think?"

It was Dennis' finest hour. He looked up straight into the headmaster's eyes, his face set in a mask of determination and excitement.

"I will be his friend, sir! I don't mind smells, sir. Honest I don't. Let him be in my room, sir. We're best friends now, sir."

Mr. Rowley nodded solemnly.

"Very well, Dennis. If Mr. Harper agrees, I think that Desmond should move into your room. And I must say," he added, turning to Desmond, "that you will be sharing with one of our finest boys."

Dennis' pride as he led his new friend out to the yard a few moments later to collect his suitcase, was indescribable. It occurred to me as I headed for the kitchen in search of bucket and disinfectant, that the little morning walks might well come to an end now. I smiled and shook my head at the ridiculous idea that entered my head then. I'd suddenly thought how disappointed the trees would be.

Chapter Nine

"You solved the mystery then, Dave?"

On my way through to the New House to pick up Tom, I'd stopped to say hello to Mark Parish, who was playing a leisurely game of draughts with Henry. The rain which had been threatening since Friday still hadn't actually arrived, but when I drew my bedroom curtains back on that Sunday morning I could see that the sky was preparing to do battle. Huge, grey reinforcements were coming in over the hills from the south-west and there was little chance of the day remaining dry. I didn't want to disappoint Tom though, so, armed with wellingtons and anorak, I had set off to dig him out and begin our walk.

"Well, yes, as a matter of fact I did, Mark. Who told you about that?"

Mark lifted an eyebrow towards the ceiling.

"Ruth. She's up there now with young Desmond, seeing to - err—this and that. Dennis is like a dog with nine bones and several tails. Keeps coming in and chatting for a bit, then rushing off and saying 'Gotta get back to my FRIEND, sir.' What about you, Dave? Nice weekend so far?"

"Yes," I said happily, "very nice, but then we've had such a nice bunch of kids here that it couldn't go wrong really."

Henry blushed with pleasure and Mark threw me an appreciative glance.

"Good," he said, "that's nice. Mind you, I can't stand Henry personally. The others are alright, but he's just a pain."

Henry grinned happily, accepting that Mark meant the exact opposite of what he'd said.

"Well you can't play draughts, sir," he countered.

"That's true," sighed Mark, looking at the little pile of captured pieces on Henry's side of the board. 'I'm pretty brilliant at everything else in the universe, but draughts—no!'

He noticed my wet-weather gear for the first time.

"Going swimming, Dave?"

I laughed, and explained about my planned walk with Tom.

"He suggested it, eh? Well, well! That's good news. Have a good walk, Dave. See you later."

As I was about to go through the swing doors, Mark stopped me with a call.

"Dave, I meant to say, what with it being your first Sunday on and all the weekenders coming back, would it help if I stayed on for a while to just show you the ropes? Just till the middle of the evening, say?"

I thought about the returning hordes. Douglas and Colin, and Martin Jarrold, and the owner of the disembodied voice, whoever he was. I'd almost forgotten that the Old House was not just a group of five—no, six now with Desmond—easily managed boys. And some of those returning would be in quite a state according to Arnold. My stomach lurched a little.

"Well, if you really wouldn't mind, Mark, it would be a terrific help."

"No problem," said Mark, turning back to his draughtboard, "even if it means having to see Henry for a bit longer."

Henry gleefully took another of Mark's pieces and added it neatly to the pile in front of him.

The New House seemed deserted at first. There was no sign of Tom or anyone else in the downstairs rooms. Upstairs, I remembered that Tom's room was the third one on the right. He was there, standing by his bed, doing up a long duffle coat. A certain wariness in his eyes when he looked round warned me not to be too matey.

"Okay, Tom?" I breezed. "Looks as if we might get wet, but I don't mind too much if you don't. Still keen on going?"

"You wanted to see how to get on to the Peak, sir?"

"Yes, that's right, I would like to. . . have a look."

"I don't mind rain, sir. It's more cosy than sunshine. I hate very hot days."

I loved very hot days.

"Ah well, all weather is, well. . . useful in one way or another, isn't it?" I said brightly.

"Yes, sir," said Tom politely.

He put a final wooden peg through its loop, and led the way out of the door, along the corridor and down the New House back stairs. Outside, the air was fresh and exciting, a patch of sky overhead shining with an unnatural pallor in the midst of a vast expanse of leaden greyness. In front of us the Peak was cardboard green against the sky, like a huge piece of theatrical scenery. The view from the top today would be amazing.

It was soon clear that the fictional device of my needing Tom to show me how to approach the Peak was fiction in his mind as well as mine. The gap in the hedge that gave access to the hill footpath was very wide and very adequately signposted.

"This is it, sir," said Tom. "You go through here."

I felt like one of those royal personages who are obliged to peer about half-wittedly in order not to rob someone of his or her piloting function.

"Through this gap you mean?" I enquired serious-ly, as though there was a wide selection of gaps to choose from.

"Yes, sir," replied Tom equally seriously, as he negotiated the low stile in front of us and stepped slightly awkwardly down onto the footpath on the other side.

Neither of us spoke as we followed the path through a small belt of scrubby trees and onto the hill itself. The slope was very steep and the path went straight up without relief between bracken at first, turning to wiry, metallic-green grass at about the half-way point. I was disgusted by how unfit I was. The duffle-coated figure in front of me was moving at a slow methodical plod that would probably take him to the top without a pause. I had run out of legs and lungs by the time I got to where the grass started. I stopped and stared out into the distance, as though the sheer magnificence of the scenery had forced me to postpone my climb for a moment. Actually, it had begun to rain and I couldn't see very far at all, so it can't have been very convincing.

"Are you alright, sir?"

Tom had stopped and was looking back at me. He sounded hardly out of breath. With a superhuman effort I controlled my wheezing for just long enough to answer him.

"Fine—great. On we go, eh?"

Fifteen gasping minutes later I reached the top and leaned gratefully against a tall metal pole that rose from the very centre of the room-sized flat area at the top of the hill. Even after resting for a few minutes it was difficult to catch my breath. The wind was a mighty, buffeting force up here and the view, wonderful as it must have been under normal circumstances, was largely obscured by cloud as rain started to sweep across the countryside, causing me to put the hood of my anorak up and turn my face away to avoid the sharp sting of the gale driven drops. Suddenly, Tom was beside me, clutching the hood of his duffle coat around his face as he tried to shout above the wind.

"My mother hates me, sir!"

This wasn't how I'd imagined it! This wasn't how these moving filmic scenes had been played out in my imagination. The significant moments of residential work should happen in warm, comfortable surroundings, not in the middle of a howling gale on top of a hill. And how should I respond to Tom's revelation? What could I say that would make any difference after all these years? It was virtually impossible to sound sensitive and understanding when you had to shout at the top of your voice. I looked at Tom's face, clenched against the noise and the cold as he waited for me to reply to him.

"Why?" I bawled.

"I don't know!" shouted Tom, "I don't know! I don't know! I don't know! I've never done anything wrong! I've asked her and I've asked my father, and they both say I've done nothing wrong! SO WHY DOES SHE HATE ME?"

It would embarrass me to record the selection of banal responses that I considered and rejected at that moment. It was flattering that Tom should have opened himself up in this way to me, but having said that, what use was I to him? There was no magic answer to that terrible question of his, and no simple comfort that would soothe away the pain that he had carried with him all his life. Suddenly the burden was too much for me. The wind, the rain, and the strain of trying to squeeze out some kind of appropriate comment was overwhelming. I was about to suggest that we went back down the hill, when, to my relief, Tom suggested it first.

"It's a bit wet and cold, sir!" he said, cupping one hand round his mouth to direct the sound. "Shall we go back?"

I nodded, and digging my hands deep into the pockets of my trousers, set off down the hill, slipping and sliding a little on the wet turf. Conditions were not so bad at the bottom of the hill, although the rain was still falling heavily. We hurried down the lane and up the long drive towards the school without speaking. Something uneasy had fallen between us and I didn't know what it was. I hadn't had time to answer Tom's last question before he suggested coming back, even if I'd known what to say. Was he waiting for me to say something else, or would it be best to keep my mouth shut? As we reached the top of the drive, I slowed down and stopped under the big fir tree. I had to say something.

"Tom," I said nervously, "just before we go in and there are lots of other people around—up there on the hill just now, when you said. . ."

"Excuse me, sir," interrupted Tom, as politely as ever, his face grave and expressionless, "can I ask you a favour?"

A drip from one of the overhanging branches fell on my nose suddenly, making me jump. I wiped it off.

"Yes, Tom," I answered encouragingly, "of course. What is it?"

There was just the faintest hint of desperation in the boy's voice as he spoke.

"Please, sir, could you not go and tell all the other staff that 'Tom's talked about his mother at last,' and, well. . . discuss it with them so they can write it in my file and all talk about what a good thing it is and . . . and all that?"

I didn't know what to say. Quite apart from the fact that my natural vanity would make it nearly impossible to avoid mentioning this 'breakthrough' to somebody, I wasn't sure how my colleagues would react to the idea of me keeping information to myself.

"You can tell Mrs. Crompton if you like, sir," added Tom quietly.

"Alright, Tom," I agreed gratefully. "I promise I'll only tell Mrs. Crompton, and I'll tell her that you don't want there to be any err. . ."

"Gossip, sir," supplied Tom.

"Err. . . quite. Yes—okay, Tom. I'll tell her—that."

"Thank you, sir. Thanks for the walk, sir."

He turned abruptly and trudged away towards the house, hunched against the rain, leaving me to wonder whether the morning had been successful or not. There had been something very unsatisfactory about that last exchange. I was glad Tom had agreed to me telling Ruth what had happened. She was wise about these things. Strange though, the whole thing. . .

A little shower of drops cut short my reverie. I hurried across to the kitchen door and stepped into the warmth and bustle of Mrs. Murchison's Sunday lunch preparations.

"Coffee, love?" said the cook.

I could have kissed her.

A few minutes later, carrying my drink in one hand and my sodden anorak at arm's length in the other, I walked into the New House dining room, intending to carry on through the swing doors and up to my flat. There was a man sitting at one of the tables flicking through a newspaper. He looked up as I appeared and spoke.

"Ah, Hiking Harper, I presume! Do favour me with your valued presence for a few solitary moments. Perhaps I shall learn why I am one client short this storm-tossed morn."

The man's tone was not pleasant. This, I presumed, was Steve Hepton, the other housefather. He was very smart, with fair wavy hair, gold-rimmed glasses, and a well-fitting grey suit. His expression and tone were lazily mocking, but there was something else there as well, something hard and seeking to hurt. I decided to be polite. Hanging my coat on the end of the radiator, I carried my coffee over to his table and sat down.

"You must be Steve Hepton," I ventured, extending my hand across the table. "I'm David Harper. Nice to meet you."

"Charmed," said Hepton, half rising and shaking my hand with elaborate formality.

"What did you mean about being one client short?" I asked.

"Only," replied Hepton, "that in your laudable rush to effect miracle cures in your free time, you failed to bear in mind that the humble staff member on duty in this establishment had no idea where master Verne had disappeared to. A trivial point I grant you, but important to me. Not being a professional eccentric like our great white chief, I prefer things to operate on a more or less ordered basis. Are you with me?"

Damn my blushing! I always felt that it put me at an immediate disadvantage. I pushed the damp hair back from my forehead and tried to think of something to say. Miracle cures? I was angry and embarrassed, but I couldn't think of anything clever to retort with.

"I'm very sorry," I said lamely. "It never occurred to me I'm afraid. It's the first time I've done anything with a boy from the other house. You're right—I should have told you what I was doing. It seemed important and I never thought. . ."

"Oh, I quite understand," interrupted Hepton smoothly. "There is to be a chapter in your autobiography entitled 'How I became the saviour of Thomas Verne in only one morning.' Why, if you take on a different boy each morning, in five weeks you will have emptied the school and we shall all be redundant. Joking apart though. . ."

I hadn't noticed any jokes.

". . . I can probably save you a great deal of time and trouble by pointing out that Master Verne is a con man of the first order and that your newly gained information that his spiritual home is a broken-down cowshed in the middle of a bog, will simply be the latest in a long line of entertaining fantasies—entertaining for our young Baron Munchausen, that is. So before you go scuttling off to scribble it all down in his file, I should bear that in mind."

I ached, I burned, I desperately wanted to tell this person what Tom had actually said on the hill that morning. That I didn't was due not to any great strength of character in me, but rather to the graphic memory of Tom's face as he had asked me not to 'gossip' about what he'd said. I took a sip of my coffee and spoke as calmly as I could.

"I honestly don't think I'm going to work any miracles," I said, "and I've no intention of 'scuttling off to scribble it all down in his file' as you put it, even if there was something to scribble, which there isn't. It's just that Mr. Rowley asked me to build up my relationship with Tom because the staff from one house can sometimes get closer to boys from the other because they don't have a disciplinary. . ."

Hepton raised his hands in mock surrender.

"Oh, please, please! Spare me the second half of the twenty-fifth Rowley lecture on child care. I have very little interest in anything said by a man who spends so much of his time carefully working out how to be spontaneously unconventional. To use an elegant phrase, what it boils down to is that Rowley is suggesting that the pathetic abilities of staff such as myself, should be supplemented—topped up as it were—by contributions from brand new members of staff such as yourself who work in a different house and have little or no knowledge of the children concerned. Mind you," he added with an abrupt and unconvincing friendliness, "I don't blame you, Dave."

Dave?

"I blame the way the place is run and the general standard of the staff."

I don't think I had ever taken such a deep dislike to someone in such a short acquaintance. What was wrong with the staff, I wondered?

"Actually," I said quietly, "I like all the staff I've met so far. They've been very helpful."

Hepton leaned his chair back on two legs and took a packet of chewing gum from his pocket. He unwrapped one of the pink strips and popped it in his mouth.

"For instance. . ?" he said through his chewing.

"Well, Ruth Crompton," I said, "She's been marvellous. . ."

"Probably fancies you," said Hepton. "I've always reckoned that Saint Ruth is probably not quite as saintly as she appears. Down in the village they say. . ."

"Then there's Mark Parish and Mike Merry," I interrupted. I didn't want to know what 'they' said about Ruth down in the village. "They seem to me very good people."

"Mark's alright," said Hepton graciously, "but old Mike's just a passenger really. No control at all. We've been carrying him since he came. Nice enough chap and all that, but too soft. Should have showed them what's what from the beginning."

"The boys seem to like him very much."

"Well, wouldn't you if someone let you do exactly what you wanted? Wise up, Dave. You've got to get on top of 'em."

Hepton would clearly have been quite happy to run down the entire staff list, favouring me with his views on each person, but I'd had enough. I got up and retrieved my anorak from the radiator.

"Anyway, I'd better go, Steve. Nice to have met you, and I'll make sure I let you know in advance next time I do anything with someone from your side."

"That would be spiffing of you," said Hepton. "Mind you, you don't want to spend too much of your own time with the lads or people will start to think you're a bit funny."

He accompanied this speech with an effeminate flap of the wrist and a suggestive laugh.

"By the way," he went on as I was about to go through the door, "the bloke to get on the right side of is Ashton, the resident rough diamond. I happen to be a bit of a dab hand when it comes to working with wood and metal, so as far as our illustrious deputy headmaster is concerned, Stephen Hepton can do very little wrong. I shall be seeing you, Dave!"

I felt poisoned. As I made my way through the Old House I met Mark at the foot of the stairs.

"I've just met Steve Hepton for the first time," I said.

"Ah, yes," Mark rubbed his chin thoughtfully. "Best not to make any bloomers with that one, Dave. He was through earlier asking if we'd seen Tom. I explained of course and said you probably hadn't thought—being new and all—but. . . well, like I said, best not to get things wrong in that direction if you can help it."

He smiled.

"Anyway, how'd you get on with our Tom. Good chat?"

"Yes," I said, "I think so, but I can't really tell you at the moment."

"Don't then!" said Mark kindly, seeing the temptation in my eyes. 'I'm just glad it went well."

Back in my flat a few minutes later, I had a wonderful view of the storm through my living room window. Hepton had upset me. In some peculiar way the violence of the weather outside gradually brought peace back to my mind.

I was very glad that Mark had offered to stay on with me until the evening. The atmosphere as boys returned in dribs and drabs through the afternoon was very jagged and tense. Each face told its own story. A few were relaxed and smiling, but several were tight with anger or unhappiness. Robert walked into the house like a small robot, his clothes still neat and tidy, his hair combed and shining with cleanliness. I spoke to him on the stairs.

"Did you have a nice weekend, Robert?"

"Yessir," said Robert through his teeth, as though he was carrying a brimming pitcher of water on his head and was afraid that an excessive movement of his jaws might result in spillage. "Stayed clean, sir."

What a sad definition of a nice weekend, I thought, as Robert continued his statuesque way upstairs, there to don his 'alternative' clothes and spectacles and become a more real Robert.

Tea was quite a noisy meal as tension was released through chattering and joking, but I sensed that Mark was as much in control as ever, and could have imposed total silence if he had thought it necessary. It was embarrassing to recall my failure to connect the behaviour of the boys with Mark's influence on that first day. I realised that I had still not heard my quietly spoken colleague raise his voice in anger yet. I wondered what it would be like. A few minutes after tea ended I found out.

The incident concerned two boys, Douglas, who had returned from his weekend in a savagely morose mood, and Desmond, the newcomer, who clung to his new friendship with Dennis even more closely as the house filled up with all these threatening personalities who belonged more than he did. Desmond was now a permanent addition to the table where Anthony, Dennis, Arnold and I sat for meals, still addressing me as though I was a military officer, and he a private soldier, even when asking for the salt to be passed. I had asked Mark earlier in the afternoon whether he thought the boy really did believe he was in the army, but Mark thought not.

"No," he said, "it's more likely that the poor lad's such a jelly inside that it makes him feel safe to pretend that the whole world's a sort of vast barracks. At least you belong if you're in the army. He won't always have to pretend that."

Desmond seemed very happy at teatime. He and Dennis were engaged in a long and ill-informed discussion about politics, in which someone called the 'Pry minster' figured heavily, and in which they agreed after considerable debate that the Queen earned about twenty pounds a week, out of which she was obliged to buy petrol for the army's tanks. Anthony took no notice. He just ate. Arnold listened indulgently with a little smile on his face. He probably knew more about politics than I did. He leaned across as tea finished and whispered to me.

"Dennis has found a friend now, hasn't he, sir?"

"Yes, Arnold," I said, "he has."

The trouble was really started by Steve Hepton, who leaned through our hatch from the kitchen after tea when there was only Douglas and I left in the dining room clearing tables, and addressed me in a loud voice.

"Bonsoir, Dave! I see Parish has got you on the menials. What's the matter? Can't you persuade the youths to do the rough?"

I managed a sort of laughing sound.

"I don't mind doing this, Steve," I said, conscious that Douglas was registering the whole conversation. "We all live here together, so why shouldn't we all help?"

His eyebrows lifted in delight.

"A philosophy, no less! Wonderful! An expert in a week. Amazing!"

He turned to go, then remembered something and turned back.

"By the way, I hear you've got a new shitter. Break out the County Council clothes pegs, eh? Good luck, Dave my boy!"

I was speechless. I knew Douglas must have heard, but I couldn't think of anything to say to him. I just hoped that he would have the compassion or—what was more likely—the sense to keep his knowledge to himself. I could read nothing in the boy's hooded eyes as he stacked the last pile of mats on the hatch and went out of the dining room. I wanted to kill Hepton. A few minutes later, I walked round into the kitchen to see if he was still there. He had gone, but through the glass door leading onto the yard I could see something else. It was Desmond, striding stiff-limbed as determinedly as his knotted shape would allow him through the puddles in the direction of the office block.

His mouth was pulled hard down at one side in contained fury and impotence. He made a grotesque, pathetic figure. I hurried out of the door and barred his way, wondering apprehensively what I would do if he didn't stop. He did stop, placing his hands with exaggerated emphasis on his bony hips. His eyes didn't meet mine at all.

"Where are you going, Desmond?" I asked gently.

"To ask the headmaster to remove me from this place as soon as possible!"

Desmond barked each word out separately, desperately striving to convey his need for a serious response to the way he was feeling. Somewhere inside him there was a baby crying. I knew it somehow.

"But what's happened, Desmond," I coaxed. "What's upset you so much?"

"Humph!" He lifted one leg and stamped it down again. A single tear was forming in one of his eyes.

"Has somebody done something to you, Desmond—or said something perhaps?"

The tear fell as words erupted jerkily from the boy's mouth.

"I will not be called Frank the shitter!"

I very nearly laughed. Not because I didn't feel very sorry for this strange boy standing before me in his ridiculous parody of an indignant pose, but because of the phrase he'd repeated. I knew where the 'shitter' part had come from, but what was the name 'Frank' supposed to convey?

"Come on, Desmond," I said, putting a hand on his shoulder, "let's go and sort this out."

Desmond didn't resist as I turned him round and steered him back in the direction of the house. Just inside the door we met Dennis, flapping his hands wildly and hopping with excitement and urgency.

"It's alright, Desmond!" he squeaked. "I've told Mr. Parish what Colin said. He's seein' 'im now in the little office. I spect he's tellin' 'im off!"

I led Desmond along the bottom corridor to a small office-like room which was kept locked and hardly ever used. From the other side of the door I could just hear a low murmur. Telling Desmond and Dennis to wait outside, I knocked and went in. There didn't seem to be much "telling off" going on. Colin, his face as white as his hair was red, sat very still on a straight-backed chair by the window, while Mark, his pipe in his mouth, was perched on the big old desk at the other side of the room, his eyes never leaving those of the boy in front of him. He took a long pull at his pipe, then spoke to Colin in a voice so low that I had to strain to hear him.

"You can go now Col," he said. "Go upstairs to your room for ten minutes and think carefully about what I've said. Off you go."

Colin rose like a wraith, and faded rather than walked out of the room. He looked bloodless. I turned to Mark.

"What on earth did you say to him, Mark?"

"Oh, just that he'd made me sad by being so cruel to Desmond. Pointed out one or two juicy little skeletons in his own cupboard that he wouldn't much enjoy having dragged out in public. Told him he was a fool to do all Douglas' dirty work for him. Asked him to make a special job of protecting Desmond. Said I was very fond of him so don't go upsetting me—those sorts of things. . ."

"So you know about Douglas hearing Steve Hepton say. . ."

Mark's face darkened.

"Yes, I do. The job's difficult enough without. . . anyway, let's get on with it. I've told Douglas to come down as soon as Colin gets back upstairs."

"So you didn't shout at Colin at all? I know that's what I'd have done."

"No point," smiled Mark. "Horses for courses, Dave. You can shout at Colin till you're blue in the face. He'll just shout back. He knows all about that. Been doing it all his life. You show him a bit of warmth and respect and he's not sure what to do. Mind you. . ." He winked. "He knows damn well I could throw him through that window if I wanted to. That helps a bit. Now Douglas. . ."

He was interrupted by a soft tap on the door. Immediately, he laid his pipe down in a glass dish on the desk, and walking quickly across the room, took up a stance looking out of the window with his back to the door.

"Come in!" he called sharply.

Douglas oiled into the room and closed the door with fastidious care behind him. His glance flickered shrewdly from my blank expression to Mark's back. There was obviously something extremely intimidating about the fact that the teacher had not turned round when he came in.

"Colin said you wanted to see me, sir."

Mark's voice when he replied was as quiet as the one he had used with Colin, but this time there was a suggestion of barely controlled fury in his tone.

"Colin was wrong, Douglas. I have absolutely no desire to see you. That is why I am not looking at you. I shall, however, be obliged to listen to your voice. I have only one question to ask you. It is true that you passed on to Colin information that you overheard in a private conversation between two members of staff, and suggested that he should use it to ridicule and deeply upset a younger boy who has only just arrived at Stapley Manor?"

Douglas licked his lips nervously. His breathing became deeper and more rapid.

"It wasn't. . ."

Mark's sudden increase in volume when he interrupted made me jump, let alone Douglas.

"Answer me!"

The boy swallowed and shifted his weight from one foot to the other.

"Yes, sir."

Mark swung round, his face almost wild with anger. He took a few steps forward until he was standing right over the boy, and shouted in a voice that must have been audible at the other end of the school grounds.

"I am going to cane you, Douglas French! I am going to cane you so hard that you'll beg for mercy!"

He bent forward until his face almost touched Douglas'.

"And what is more, I shall enjoy every single bleat that you make as I do it! Understand, bully-boy?"

Douglas, who was looking positively dehydrated, nodded feebly.

Mark turned abruptly away from the boy and started to hunt feverishly through an open drawer in the other side of the desk.

"Where the hell is my cane?" he muttered, pulling the drawer out bodily and emptying its contents with a crash on top of the desk. There was no cane among them. He turned his attention to the cupboard against the wall by the window but was equally unsuccessful there. Grunting with the effort, he heaved a filing cabinet away from the wall and peered round the back of it. There was something deeply frightening about the way his frustration and fury increased as the search continued. He looked everywhere that a cane could possibly be concealed, hissing oaths through clenched teeth as he tore wildly around the room. Meanwhile, Douglas, who must have been inwardly computing the effect of all this extra frustration when Mark did finally find his cane, had turned a sort of yellowy-green colour. His fingers plucked fitfully at the hem of his jumper.

"I can't find the damn thing!"

Mark stood in the centre of the room, clenching and unclenching his fists, as if tempted to use them instead of the elusive cane.

"Get out!" he suddenly shouted at the terrified boy. "Get out while you've still got your miserable skin! And think yourself lucky I couldn't find my blasted stick! If I hear of you doing anything like this again, I won't use a cane—I'll use a blasted chair! Now get out!"

Douglas got out.

As the door closed, Mark staggered over to the window and slumped down onto the chair that Colin had used earlier.

"Well!" he gasped, taking out a handkerchief and mopping his temples. 'That's worn me out. I must be getting old.''

I felt quite exhausted myself.

"I'm just glad you didn't find your cane," I said. "You'd 've nearly killed him!"

Mark smiled weakly. "What cane?" he said. "I haven't got a cane. I've never had a cane. I'm not allowed to use a cane. I made the cane up. Tell you what though—I'll bet you all next month's salary that our friend Douglas feels as if he's had it five times over.''

''Yes,'' I replied, ''I think you're probably right. . .''

The rest of the evening was remarkably peaceful. Colin and Douglas were keeping a very low profile, and the rest of the boys seemed suitably impressed by ''Mr. Parish going spare'' as Henry called it. Mark left at about eight o'clock, his departure going unnoticed by most of the boys, and I certainly wasn't going to go out of my way to tell them. Bedtime was a very civilised affair, despite the fact that the weekenders had returned, and as I made a final tour of the corridors, switching off lights and saying goodnight, I felt a little glow of satisfaction. My first week as a residential social worker had been very difficult at times, but I was still there, and things were looking very interesting. I still had the George Ashton problem to contend with, but in time. . . .

I reached Arnold's room. There was something I wanted to ask Arnold.

''Arnold,'' I said, after I'd tucked him in, ''can I ask you a question?''

''Yes, sir,'' responded the boy, his resonant voice muffled by bedclothes.

''Why,'' I asked, lowering my voice, ''did Desmond get called 'Frank' when they were taking the mickey out of him?''

''Because of the shape of his head, sir,'' said Arnold.

I considered this piece of information.

''I don't understand, Arnold.''

''His head's sort of square, like Frankenstein's monster on the films, sir. Frank's short for Frankenstein. It's not really accurate anyway, sir, because it was the scientist who was called Frankenstein, not the monster, and anyway Mary Shelley's monster wasn't anything like the one on the films, sir, was it?''

''Errr. . . no, Arnold, you're quite right, and thank you very much.''

''Goodnight, sir.''

''Goodnight, Arnold.''

I went to bed, warmed by a delicious sense of anticipation. Tomorrow I would see Annie.

Chapter Ten

Catching a bus outside the grocer's the next morning was a strange experience. It had been such an intense week that, despite my very real excitement about going back to Tunbridge Wells and seeing Annie, it was almost impossible to stop my mind dwelling on the people and situations that I was leaving behind at Stapley Manor. A hurried conversation with Ruth Crompton just before leaving hadn't helped. I'd met her in the yard on my way out, and stopped to give here a brief account of my walk with Tom, concluding with a mention of his anxiety about being discussed as a 'case'. As my green, single-decker chariot lumbered away from Stapley towards the main road, I remembered the troubled look on her face when I'd finished.

"Of course it's a good thing that he's started to open up," she'd said. "What worries me is that he's released so little of what he really feels. Now that the unblocking process has started, I have a feeling there could be one almighty explosion in the offing, and as you're the one he's opened up to, it could well happen in your direction."

This bothered me. I found it difficult to imagine Tom, grave and contained, 'exploding' in any sense. The contrast would be disturbingly, frighteningly bizarre. Fascinating as well, though.

I thought of Dennis and his new friend, and of Arnold who still had no friend. I wondered if I would ever forge a relationship with Martin Jarrold who still couldn't forgive me for not being Mr. Boon. How was Twinkle doing over in the New House, I mused, and what was Mrs. Hepton like? What on earth could Henry and James have ever done to be sent away from home? Was anyone actually doing anything to help fat Anthony? Who was the unknown owner of the disembodied voice? Perhaps when I got back I could make a list of all the boys and. . .

The back of the bus hit a bump, sending me up like a jack-in-a-box from my seat. I plummeted down, distracted at last from my almost feverish absorption in things that I was supposed to be having time off from. Outside, a watery sun was doing a feeble job of illuminating the scenery. I suddenly realised that we'd travelled several miles, and this was the first time I'd noticed anything out of the window. Usually I looked at everything—maybe it would be a good idea if Colin and Douglas didn't share a room, because then. . .

I shook my head and blinked hard. This was ridiculous! Never in my life had my attention been held in such a vice-like grip, and this was after only seven days! Half an hour away and already I was fretting to get back and make sure that without my indispensable presence things hadn't 'gone wrong'. I determinedly thought of Annie, and by the time we were a couple of miles north of Mayfield she was definitely winning. Later, as I got off the bus at the stop opposite the church of King Charles the Martyr in Tunbridge Wells, Stapley Manor had become a vague memory and all I wanted was to see her again. We had arranged to meet in the Pantiles, a regency shopping parade that we were both very fond of, and the site of the flat which I had occupied until moving to Stapley. I saw her at the far end of the tree lined walkway, her nose up against a shop window. I managed to get right up to her and tap her on the shoulder before she turned round.

I'd forgotten how warm Annie was, and how much I needed someone to hold and get close to. We were wrapped round each other for nearly a minute before either of us spoke. At last Annie stood back, holding both of my hands in hers, and studied my face with her head on one side, her eyes shining with happiness.

"Hello, David," she said. "We're together again."

My mouth was stretched so tightly into a huge, silly grin that I coud hardly speak.

"Hello, Annie," I managed at last. "You're my friend."

I knew she would understand what I meant.

"Yes," she said quietly, "we are friends as well as everything else, aren't we?" She smiled like a small child. "Do you still want to marry this friend of yours?"

"Oh, yes," I answered, "from the point of view of tax alone. . ."

The rest of the day was as near perfect as it could be, but by the evening I was becoming slightly concerned. Not even the ghost of an argument all day as we walked and talked and ate.

"Ah, yes," I thought, as we walked into the comfortable buzz and clink of the King's Head that evening, "but we haven't got onto the business of Annie applying for the housemother's job yet."

For some reason neither of us had brought the subject up all day. Perhaps we were afraid of disturbing the peace. We'd talked about my job and the people I'd met—the things that had happened. It had been wonderful being able to share everything with someone who really wanted to know how I felt. I hadn't been able to resist the thought of how perfect it would be if Annie was there every day, involved and concerned with the same people and things. Surely she would want to come. It would mean we could be together.

"Annie," I said, when we were settled with our drinks in one of the little alcoves, "have you thought some more about what I told you? The job I mean—have you decided whether to apply or not?"

"David," said Annie very softly, "do you realise that since we met this morning you haven't asked me a single question about the job that I'm doing?"

"But it's. . ."

"Don't get me wrong," interrupted Annie, "I'm not saying that I mind particularly. I'm just trying to make the point that my job—what I do—is very important to me. It's not just a question whether to apply for a different job, it's whether to stop nursing as well. Do you understand what I'm saying?"

"Of course," I said tetchily. "I'm not stupid."

Neither of us said anything for a moment. I fished in my drink for an imaginary speck, then spoke without looking up.

126

"So, what you're saying is that you aren't going to try for the job?"

Leaning back, Annie swept her hair behind her shoulders in exasperation.

"You haven't understood, have you? You haven't even tried to understand! There are two of us sitting here, and we're equally important. I'm not just a mirror for you to admire David Harper in. We're going to be together anyway eventually and I just don't want to make any decisions now that I'll regret later on. I know you're all wrapped up in working with these boys, and that's great! I'm really glad you've found something that interests you so much, but I'm in the middle of my career and I've got no particular reason to believe that I'd be happier, or even as happy, doing what you're doing. If it comes to that, why don't you come and train to be a nurse then we could both do what I do!"

"That's just silly!" I said petulantly. "Let's at least talk sense if we're going to talk at all. I've never had even the remotest interest in taking temperatures and bathing bedsores."

This deliberately absurd summary of nursing functions did not go down at all well with Annie, who had always taken her profession very seriously indeed. She leaned forward across the table so that she could inject all the annoyance she was feeling into a whisper that was inaudible to the other people in the pub.

"And I haven't the remotest interest in supervising the disposal of little boys' dirty underpants while you swan around having meaningful conversations on the tops of hills! I take it that those would be our respective roles?"

I debated inwardly whether to be deeply hurt and upset by this comment. I decided not. Annie crying and vulnerable I could handle. Annie angry was a different proposition altogether. I opted for gaining the initiative by making a mature and responsible peace move. Gripping my pint glass resolutely in both hands I looked steadily into the angry grey eyes before me and adopted a sensible but conciliatory tone.

"Look, let's not argue, Annie. I was a bit thought-less. . ."

"Correct."

With a superhuman effort I continued.

"But there's no use in wasting the time we've got together in arguing. I've got to go back tomorrow. Look—how about this. . .?"

"Yes?" said Annie warily, tilting her face to one side and studying me suspiciously through narrowed eyes. "What?"

"How about you coming down for a weekend just to get the feel of the place and meet the boys, and, well. . . at least consider the idea? And if you decide it really doesn't appeal to you, then. . ."

"You'll say, 'Fine, Annie darling. I respect your decision and accept it absolutely and I won't go on and on about it for the rest of our lives and I won't sulk or get angry, even if I feel as if I want to?" That is what you'll say, isn't it, David darling?"

"Errr. . . yes, something like that."

I tried to keep a straight face, but Annie's eyes, wide open now in mock enquiry, made it impossible to prevent a smile of self-conscious acknowledgement from spreading across my face. She knew me so well.

"Well, I'll try not to sulk or get angry anyway, Annie. I really will. What do you say?"

"Alright." She smiled and shrugged. "I'd like to stay for a weekend in any case, but I'm not even thinking about applying before then, and I'm not making any promises. Okay?"

"Okay," I said happily, relieved that the conflict was not going to be prolonged. "That's fine. Let's have another drink."

Saying goodbye to Annie outside the hospital the next morning was awful. At that moment I think that for two pins either of us would have done almost anything that meant we could stay together. As always in these situations, however, two is actually an awful lot of pins, and we went our respective ways dutifully but very sadly.

Later, on the way back to Stapley in Steve's battered old Cortina, I described the problems I'd been having with repairs in the Old House.

"There's one locker," I said plaintively to Steve, "that's had it in for me ever since I got there. It's determined not to have its door back on whatever I do. I glue it, and put hinges on it, and measure it up, and screw it on, then I tiptoe away as quietly as I can, but by the time I get to the door it's sagged, or split, or come undone, and I have to start all over again. It does it deliberately, Steve, I swear it does. Inanimate objects hate me.''

"Why not just accept you can't do it?" said Steve practically. "Go and tell this Ashton bloke you're useless at that bit of the job, and ask him to show you how to do it. Easy!"

"Mmmm. . . I suppose so."

Privately I thought that George Ashton almost certainly reckoned I was useless at every other bit of the job as well. I would find it very difficult to ask him for help. It occurred to me once more that Ruth Crompton and the headmaster must have knocked the deputy head to the floor, knelt on his chest, and started pulling all his teeth out before he would have agreed to my appointment. Steve was saying something else.

"After all, let's face it—you told 'em you'd be able to do it and you can't. So you're the one who's in the wrong, aren't you?"

"Yes, Steve," I acknowledged miserably. "Why can't you be a flattering, sycophantic sort of friend?"

Steve smiled grimly.

"And risk getting beaten up by Annie? You must be joking!"

It was teatime when I arrived back at school. There was no one in sight as Steve swung the car round expertly in the yard, dropped me off, and sped away with a wave in the direction of the drive. I stood quite still for a moment in the middle of the yard after the car had gone, just listening. Faintly, I could hear the murmur of voices and an occasional burst of laughter from the dining rooms of the two houses. I was back. I felt in my stomach that flutter of fear and excitement that was already becoming a familiar sensation, and realised that I was actually looking forward to work the following morning. It was a pleasurable feeling, but it wasn't allowed to last long. As I crossed the tarmac towards the Old House, Steve Hepton came out of the kitchen door, swept a glance around the open space in front of him, and called out as he spotted me.

"Dave! A word in your shell-like."

I waited as the suave, nattily dressed figure walked towards me. I knew somehow that I wouldn't like what I was about to hear. The expression on Hepton's face as he approached was one of anticipatory relish. He stopped in front of me, one hand in a trouser pocket, the other cupped easily just below his chest - like an actor.

"Heard the vehicle," he said, "so I thought I'd just come out and check. You see, we have a teeny-weeny problem on our hands, Dave, and you ought to know about it in view of the fact that you have taken over young Tom's case."

"I haven't. . ."

"The fact is that Master Verne is no more."

A chill of fear rippled through me.

"What do you mean?"

"I mean," said Hepton, savouring every word, "that after your miracle mission to the top of yonder mountain on Sunday, Tom became progressively more withdrawn and uncommunicative. He made a small excursion out of his self-constructed shell to ask me if he might be allowed to visit your good self. That was yesterday morning. I informed him of course that despite your generous use of free time on his behalf on the previous day, you were now off the premises and unavailable for whatever it was he required you for. At lunchtime yesterday he simply evaporated and has failed to return since."

For a moment I felt only relief. I'd thought he meant that Tom was dead. A feeling of alarm followed as I adjusted to what Hepton had just told me.

"You mean he's been out all night?"

"Absolutely."

"And no one's got any idea where he is?"

"None whatsoever. The police have been informed. The deputy head and poor old Mike have been scurrying around the countryside on and off for the past twenty-four hours hoping to locate the boy. George Ashton is out looking at this very moment. What a to-do, eh, Dave? It rather looks as if his revelation to you that his life's ambition is to live down a giant rabbit hole or whatever, has not had a remarkably beneficial effect."

"You mean it's my fault that he's gone?"

It was obviously not Hepton's way to make comments directly, especially negative ones.

"Good heavens, no, Dave. It's probably pure coincidence that, having never run away in the past, he should do so after you, a new and inexperienced member of staff, go out

130

of your way to attempt to succeed where the rest of us have failed."

If I hadn't been so worried about Tom I would have punched Hepton on the nose at that point. If he'd just been plain angry I don't think I would have minded so much, but the resentment that was clearly in him expressed itself so cuttingly that it provoked an equal reaction. I turned and went into the house without saying another word. Tea was still going on as I climbed the main stairs and let myself into my flat. There was no one else around thank goodness. The air inside the flat was very cold and slightly moist. I turned my convector heater on and made sure all the windows were securely shut. I didn't want to get chilled tonight and start one of those flu bouts that I seemed so prone to. In the bedroom I found my hot water bottle at the bottom of the wardrobe. It was the work of a few minutes to heat some water and push the bottle down between the sheets of my bed to get rid of any traces of dampness. With the water left in the kettle I poured myself a black coffee and took it over to the armchair, positioned so that I could look out of the window and see the hills across the valley. Sitting and sipping at the hot dark liquid I wondered if Tom was out there somewhere, hiding in a corner with his unhappiness, desperately trying to postpone the explosion that Ruth had predicted. He'd been out all night. No water bottle, no hot drinks, nothing to warm or comfort him. Was it my fault? Did it matter anyway? Successive waves of guilt and worry flooded through me as I sat on and on watching the daylight fade into darkness, until all I could see in front of me were the stars in the sky and the lights of Stapley twinkling yellow and orange down in the valley.

I looked at the luminous dial on my watch. It was eight-thirty. I'd been sitting in the same position for three hours. I got up and stretched painfully. Time to put some lights on. At the exact moment when my finger pushed the switch down, the first window smashed. The correspondence was so precise in fact, for one confused and shocked moment I thought that by some crazy law of science I'd never heard of, the two events were causally linked. Then I noticed the large stone which had come to rest in the middle of the carpet, surrounded by splinters and slices of glass. As I bent down to pick the stone up, panicking and unable to make sense of what had happened, my heart hammering wildly against my chest, a second window seemed to explode in front of me, and another missile, a half brick this time, narrowly missed my left foot as it thumped onto the floor and rolled heavily to a standstill just behind the spot where I was kneeling. It never occurred to me to turn the lights off. I was utterly paralysed by the situation, or I would have realised that my attacker had been presented with a perfect target as soon as I pressed the switch. Hardly realising what I was doing, I rose slowly to my feet and backed in real terror towards the sink, my attention so firmly fixed on the remaining windows that I forgot the existence of the half brick, and stumbled back with a crash into the hard wooden edge of the draining board, just as a third window burst in pieces into the room. From the pitch darkness outside someone was crashing brutally through the outside of my little lighted cockpit. It was as though they were assaulting a space right inside my head. Unable to cope any longer, I crouched by the sink, my arms wrapped over the top of my head and my eyes tight shut as the two remaining windows fell in quick succession. After that there was a long ringing silence. I opened my eyes after a minute or so and looked from side to side of the room, only my eyeballs moving as I took in the extent of the damage. Glass, mud and stones were everywhere. All five of the big main windows were demolished, the little ones at the top had somehow escaped harm. As my brain ground slowly back into action, I reached up the wall with one arm and flicked the light switch off. The darkness was an immediate comfort. Now I was on equal terms with my invisible attacker. He could see me no better than I could see him. Not as well perhaps. I stood up and edged warily over to the window, crunching glass into the carpet as I went. Peering down through a jagged edged hole in one of the panes, I could see the area around the flower beds and the tennis court quite clearly, the light from the Old and New House games rooms filtering through closed curtains and casting a gentle orange glow over the grounds at the back of the house. There was no one to be seen. He, she or it must have retreated into the trees and bushes at the other side of the tennis court, or simply walked round the angle of the building and out of sight. Why hadn't anyone come out of the french windows at the back to find out what was going on? They must have heard the glass smashing. I turned away from the window and stood for a moment, unsure what to do next. Whatever it was, I would need to calm down first. My heart had slowed its frantic rate a little but I was shaking all over. Incredibly, the whole incident had lasted for no more than thirty seconds from the breaking of the first window to the last, but I felt as if I'd been under siege for hours. Strangely enough, it never crossed my mind that I might know the person responsible for what had just happened, although why I thought a total stranger would be interested in lobbing half bricks so deliberately in my direction I couldn't have said.

The sudden sound of my doorbell ringing nearly made me jump out of the window. Nightmare images flashed through my imagination of wild-eyed axemen crouched on the other side of the door, waiting for me to appear so that they could bury their blades in my skull.

"You're an idiot!" I told myself in a fierce whisper. "It'll just be someone coming up to find out what's happening. Mad axemen don't ring the doorbell like that. Turn the light on and open the door!"

I didn't dare switch on the living room light. Instead, I reached round the bedroom door and turned that one on. With the door pushed right back, it illuminated the little area just inside my front door quite adequately. I took a deep breath, turned the sprung handle on the Yale lock, and slowly pulled the door open.

It was Tom. Dirty, dishevelled, and with blazing, pleading eyes, but undoubtedly Tom. I knew straight away that it was he who had broken all my windows. Most normal people would probably have known that already. For some moments neither of us spoke. Tom's mouth was working and twitching silently as though he couldn't manage to turn his feelings and thoughts into a proper form of words. I said nothing because I couldn't work out what I was. Victim, friend, member of staff, outraged householder—what was I?

"I ran away, sir."

It was Tom who broke the silence first. His eyes, wide and staring, never left mine. I nodded almost imperceptibly. Tom went on, his voice breathy and catching with emotion.

"I hid in the—the camp store, sir. I know how to work the lock on the door. There's a window up there. I watched—waited till you came back, then when it was dark I—I came out and collected together some stones and things round by the tennis court, and then when you switched your light on I started smashing your windows, sir. It was me. I—I smashed your windows, sir. . . ."

I hardly heard the words. It was Tom's barely contained grief that communicated itself overwhelmingly. Added to the still-present effects of the shock I had just had, it created an emotional upheaval in me that was demanding urgent release. Aware that I was about to burst into tears myself, I turned away from the boy and walked back into the living room, twisting my hands together in front of me as I searched desperately for resources from somewhere to handle what was going on around and inside me. Pausing to flick the light on, I picked my way through the debris, removed a sliver of glass from the armchair, and sat down, grateful, despite the cold, for the fresh night air blown on to my face through the gaping holes in the glass. Tom had followed me. He came and stood beside my chair, his tall figure sagging tiredly inside the now disreputable duffle coat.

"I broke your windows because. . ."

Tom broke off as something in him fought to weep its way out. He swallowed two or three times, his eyes screwed tight shut as he regained sufficient control to speak again.

"I broke your windows because—I wanted you to know—I wanted you to know how much—how much. . ."

Suddenly the dam burst irretrievably. Tom sank to his knees as great sobs shook the whole of his body and giant tears welled up in his eyes, to roll unchecked down his white, crumpled face. Instinctively I put my arms out towards him. As soon as my hands touched his shoulders, he moved towards me like a small child, his whole body curling and rolling over the side of the chair into my lap, until he was coiled into as tight a ball as his sixteen year old body would allow, his hands clutching fistfuls of my pullover, his face pressed into my chest. A surge of tearful anger swept hotly through me as I felt all those years of uncomprehending misery and hurt shaking themselves in great gouts of grief from the trembling body that I cradled so inadequately in my arms. It wasn't fair! Whoever was or wasn't to blame, it just wasn't fair! I was unable to hold my own tears back as I sensed, more clearly than words could ever have communicated, the sort of suffering that Tom had endured and never learned to express since things had gone so badly wrong when he was a small baby. I bent my head to the top of his, and wept for him as he wept for himself. It was in this position that George Ashton and Mike Merry found us when they walked into the flat a few minutes later.

Tom was no longer sobbing, just lying quietly against me breathing evenly. Most of the tension had worked its way out now and his body felt quite relaxed. My emotion was rapidly giving way to exhaustion. I think I could quite easily have dropped off to sleep on the spot. Sensing that someone had come in, I raised my head wearily to see who was there. I couldn't tell what the deputy head was thinking by the expression on his face. I didn't care much at that moment.

"Blimey! What a mess!"

Mike Merry was inspecting the windows.

"Who broke 'em?" said George Ashton conventionally. His reaction to the whole scene had so far appeared remarkably impassive. Was he really only concerned about the windows?

Tom raised his head at the question. Uncurling himself methodically, he climbed off my knees, passed an unavailing hand over his dirty, tear-streaked face and took up a stance beside the deputy, hands deep in his duffle coat pockets. Side by side they studied the wreckage of my windows.

"I broke 'em, sir," said Tom, his voice surprisingly steady.

"I see," replied the deputy, equally calmly. "Well, you'll have to pay for 'em then, won't you?"

"Yes, sir," said Tom, "and then there's punishment, sir."

"Punishment?"

"For breaking the windows, sir. It's against the rules to break windows."

"That's true," the man nodded. "I'll have to work out some jobs to fill up your spare time over the next few weeks, won't I? You can start by helping to put these windows in tomorrow lunchtime. You're going to end up with no money and less energy after all this, my lad."

"Yes, sir," said Tom, sounding suitably contrite.

I realised suddenly that the bond between George Ashton and Tom Verne was strong and deep-rooted, for all that the boy had never found it possible to really open up before. Mike Merry was grinning like a Cheshire cat.

"Then there's the running away," he said. "Have to see the Head about that. He'll probably cane you, Tom."

"Yes, sir," said Tom, nodding in his old, grave fashion. "He probably will—or shoot me, sir."

"Or shoot you, yes!" said Mike, apparently delighted at the prospect.

"So, just before Mr. Merry takes you down and sorts you out some food, and I take Mr. Harper out and buy him several large drinks, the question is," added the deputy, folding his arms and looking at Tom from under his thick brows, "bearing in mind all that—was it worth it?"

Tom still looked awful—pale and tired and dirty. But there was a hint of new light in his eyes as he looked across at me for a moment, then back to George Ashton.

"Yes, sir," he said, quietly but firmly, "it was."

That evening signalled a new beginning in my relationship with George Ashton. Over the promised several large drinks he made me tell him the whole story of what had happened with Tom, belying his rather gnarled persona by turning out to be a sensitive and interested listener. With the assistance of the alcohol, I also plucked up the courage to confess that I had not been entirely honest about my practical abilities, an item of information which obviously came as no surprise to the deputy who offered to give me some lessons in basic repair skills if I was interested.

Just after last orders had been called, George leaned back against the polished oak panels of The Old Moon, and addressed me in the tone of one who has been mellowed by best bitter.

"Y'know," he said, "I wasn't sure if you were gonna make it at Stapley, and I don't doubt you and I will have our differences as time goes by, but I tell you what. . ."

He leaned forward and lowered his voice.

"After tonight, I'm damned glad I talked the others into offering you the job!"

Chapter Eleven

It was almost a relief the next day to get back to the routine difficulties involved in working with the group. Any inflated ideas I might have had about my abilities as a residential worker after the incident with Tom, would have been swiftly punctured by the events of the morning. My problems concerned two lads in particular, the fattest boy and the largest boy in the Old House respectively.

The fattest boy, Anthony Fitton, complied with most routine demands without argument, albeit gracelessly, but he showed absolutely no enthusiasm whatsoever for anything that could not be consumed. I had found him a featureless, unattractive personality in the short time I'd known him, but I had certainly never suspected that he could become violent. By the time breakfast was over on this Wednesday morning, I knew just how dangerous he could be.

The incident started when I suddenly realised that, yet again, Dennis was the server on our table. As he rose after grace and started weaving his way towards the hatch to collect the cereals, I thought back over the meals I had been present for in the last week or so. Yes, there was no doubt about it—Dennis had been the server on our table on every single occasion. As the first two bowls of cornflakes arrived, and Dennis departed unsteadily for more, I leaned to one side and spoke quietly to Arnold.

"Arnold, how often are you supposed to change servers?"

"Every day, sir," whispered Arnold co-operatively. "We change over every day."

"Yes, but you don't on this table, do you, Arnold? Dennis always does it. At least—he's done it every time I've been here. Why's that?"

Arnold frowned in thought.

"I don't really know, sir. I think he just sort of does it, and we just sort of let him because. . . I don't know, sir."

He shook his head over this problem that could not be solved by mathematics, then shrugged unconcernedly.

"Anyway, sir, I don't mind taking my turn. I'll do the rest of today if you want, sir."

"Well, just hold on a moment, Arnold," I said, looking round at the other boys seated at our table, "let's have a think."

Everybody was supplied with cereal now. Dennis and Desmond, who had got theirs last, were busy adding sugar and milk, some of which reached their bowls and some of which missed badly. Anthony was trying to scrape the glaze off the bottom of his bowl, while keeping one beady little eye on the plate of bread and butter which had somehow ended up nearer to his place than anyone else's. Who should I choose to break the mould and take over serving for the rest of the day? Anthony glanced up suddenly and saw me looking at him. A fat gleam came into his eye.

"You goin' to make Dennis stand up on a chair an' answer questions like Mr. Boon used to, sir?"

Annoyance filled me immediately.

"Why would I want to do something like that, Anthony?" I asked sharply.

Anthony's eyes disappeared into his head as his face was split by a wide smile of relish. His shoulders quivered with silent laughter.

"So funny!" he squeaked. "Standin' up on the chair lookin' stupid! Go on, sir—ask 'im some questions!"

There was something about Anthony's manner that infuriated me. How dare he assume that I would gain some kind of satisfaction from humiliating Dennis? What did that say about his opinion of me? I wanted to penetrate the fat, selfish exterior—to make him aware that I had power over him. He had abandoned his cereal bowl now and was just stretching out a paw towards the bread and butter. I reached across the table and abstracted the plate neatly.

138

"You're not having any more of that!" I announced, putting the plate down beside my table mat. "Just for once you're going to leave a bit for others. Also, you can do the serving for the rest of the day, starting now. Clear these bowls up and get the plates from the hatch. Go on! Move!"

The smile had vanished from Anthony's face as soon as I moved the bread and butter. His eyes flashed angrily. I was impingeing on the most important area in his life.

"Gimme some bread and butter!" he hissed venomously.

I was aware that the noise on the other tables had stopped. They were all listening. If only I could prevent the nervousness I felt from coming through in my voice.

"I've told you you're not having any more bread and butter, Anthony. I've also told you to get on with the serving. I suggest you do what you're told or you'll get no more breakfast at all."

The hate in Anthony's eyes was indescribable.

"Dennis does the servin'!"

"Exactly," I replied. "He does it too much. Now it's your turn. No one on this table is getting any more food unless you get it, so if you want us all to sit here doing nothing until it's time for jobs, that's up to you—but just remember it's your choice."

I turned towards the other tables.

"The rest of you can get on with your eating. It's got nothing to do with anyone else."

The noise on the other tables resumed, increased in volume now as the boys reacted to the drama that was being enacted on my table. I groaned inwardly. How was I going to resolve this situation? Anthony was sitting solidly in his chair, his eyes fixed on the bread and butter, his lips pushed forward in a pout of stubborn refusal. Arnold and Dennis and Desmond were all wistfully watching toast and fried tomatoes being eaten on the other tables.

"I don't mind servin', sir," said Dennis hopefully.

"I'm afraid that's not the point, Dennis," I replied, folding my arms and trying to sound calm and adult. "I wouldn't mind serving either, but I've asked Anthony to do it, and if he doesn't, no one will."

The seconds passed. Anthony didn't move. I was perspiring with anger and embarrassment. Suddenly I couldn't stand it any longer. If he wouldn't move, I'd make him move! Pushing my chair back, I got up and moved round the table until I was standing behind the round figure, still plumped immovably on his chair.

"You are going to do the serving!" I said firmly, and laid my hand on his arm, intending to move him physically out of his seat.

The point of the blade just missed me. Anthony had swung round blindly as soon as I touched him, lunging in the general direction of my stomach with his left hand, which contained Desmond's breakfast knife. Whether he really intended to stab me or not I don't know. Perhaps he deliberately missed. Whatever his actual intention, the effect on me was profound. I had never been physically assaulted in my life. Somehow I managed to grab his wrists and shake the knife from his left hand onto the floor. My knees had turned to jelly and there was a throbbing pain behind my eyes as I held him down on his chair and wondered what to do next. From some other table I heard that same anonymous voice speaking very quietly.

"Go on, Ant. Fix 'im good."

"Shall I take Anthony, Mr. Harper?"

Oh joy! It was Ruth. She was standing in the open doorway between the games room and the dining room.

"You might as well, Mrs. Crompton," I said, controlling the strain in my voice as best I could. "He's certainly no use to us here at the moment."

There was dead silence from the rest of the boys now. What was it about people like Ruth and Mark? I felt a sudden stab of depression. Why couldn't I command that kind of respect?

"Come on, Anthony," said Ruth quietly, "come with me."

I released Anthony's wrists and stood back. He climbed out of his chair and walked straight over to Ruth, who guided his ample form through the door and out of sight. The noise restarted. Arnold whispered diplomatically to me.

"Shall I do Anthony's serving for him, sir, seeing as he's not here?

"Yes, Arnold," I said, not caring what happened at that particular moment, "you do that."

"You handled it badly, David," said Ruth ten minutes later.

"I know," I replied dismally. "I knew at the time really. I just wanted to get at Anthony he made me so mad. And his fatness annoys me. I know that doesn't make any sense, but it's true!"

We were standing outside the kitchen, watching Anthony work as hard as his bulk would allow on the yard sweeping. Jobs had been reallocated on Monday, and this was his daily task until next week. He found me two minutes ago to apologise and promise that he would do the server's job for the rest of the day.

"I know exactly what you mean, David," said Ruth after a moment's thought, "but that's just the point. With a boy like Anthony you can't afford to operate out of your own anger. He's as stubborn as they come, and quite vicious if he's cornered. You have to find a way to use his momentum, rather like in Judo I suppose. Mr. Rowley's a past master at the art."

"Well," I said, "at least his apology sounded real enough just now. He seemed quite anxious to get back on good terms with me."

Ruth sighed.

"Yes, he did, didn't he? I'm afraid it's more to do with food than anything else, actually. Old Anthony would do almost anything to keep the grub coming in. He comes from a very big family with next to no money—dad's a scrap merchant. I'm sure he really did have to fight for his share sometimes. I've never known him actually to pick up a knife like that before though."

I shivered involuntarily.

"If it's any consolation to you, David, I doubt very much if he was making a calculated attempt to stab you, more a sort of lashing out. Shows how careful you've got to be, doesn't it?"

If that knife had hit me, I reflected, it wouldn't have been much of a consolation to know that Anthony was only 'lashing out.' Still, I didn't want to make too much fuss about the incident. Ruth seemed to regard it as being all part of the day's work. Presumably I would feel the same in time, unlikely as it seemed.

"Anyway," went on Ruth briskly, "as usual I came over to do one thing and ended up doing something completely different. I actually wanted to speak to you about something—well, two things really. First of all, I heard about

141

Tom and the windows and everything last night, and I wanted to say. . ."

She looked down and gave a little embarrassed laugh.

"I don't really know what I wanted to say. Just, I suppose, that I'm glad it was you he came back to, and. . . well, I'm overjoyed that the unblocking process has begun, and—and I'm sorry about your windows!"

We both burst into laughter at the conclusion of Ruth's feeble attempt to communicate her feelings. It didn't matter. I knew what she was trying to say.

"The other thing," said Ruth, still smiling to herself, "was about the housemother's job I mentioned to you. You did talk to Annie about it, did you?"

"Oh, yes," I said somewhat over-earnestly, "she's really interested—well, she is interested, but. . ."

"But she doesn't know whether she wants to give up her own career to do a job she doesn't know anything about. Right?"

"Err. . . yes, that's about it," I acknowledged, taken aback by the accuracy of Ruth's assessment of the situation. "She says she'd like to come and stay for a weekend before even thinking about applying, and even then. . . I don't know. . ."

"Well, you mustn't bully her, David. Let her come for an ordinary weekend, and then—hold on a minute!"

Ruth rubbed a cheekbone with her finger as an idea occurred to her.

"What about a camp, David? Why not take the group away for a weekend and ask Annie to come with you? You could go this coming weekend if the forecast is reasonable. Might be a bit chilly, but you could light a fire, take plenty of blankets - could be a lot of fun."

"What—you mean with tents?" I asked doubtfully.

She laughed. "Well, they could come in useful on a camp - yes."

"Mmmm, I don't know. . ."

Just at that moment Anthony loomed into close view, brush in hand, his little eyes shifting with unaccustomed anxiety.

"Think about it," said Ruth. "I'll see you later."

She walked away in the direction of the offices.

"'Scuse me, sir," squeaked Anthony, "I've done my job. Can you check it for me please, sir?"

I looked at our section of the yard. It was spotless. I looked at Anthony again. He was a very doleful little fat person.

"Is it alright, sir? I done it as well as I could."

Thinking about Annie had made me feel generous.

"It's perfect!" I enthused. "Absolutely perfect! Well done, Anthony. You may go and put your brush away."

He started to rotate his bulk, then stopped.

"An' I'm sorry about smornin', sir. I will be the server on our table."

"I told you before, Anthony, I forgive you. It's all in the past now."

"So I'll be allowed to eat same as usual at dinner, will I, sir?"

"Yes, Anthony."

A deep sigh of relief escaped the podgy lips. A bright, almost spiritual light appeared in the close-set eyes.

"Oh good, sir! 'Cause it's jam puddin' today."

Back in the Old House I encountered my second problem of the morning. Martin Jarrold, the oldest boy in the group, had been surly and unco-operative since that morning when I had stopped him on the stairs and forced him to at least make a pretence of washing. There was no conflict in that particular area now. He slouched grimly from his bedroom to the shower block in his pyjamas each morning, coming back slightly wetter but no less grim a few minutes later. There was still no real contact between us though, and more than one confrontation had nearly ended with him raising his fist to me. Frankly, he scared me. Not only was he much more powerfully built than I was, but he also had a very quick mind. Mark Parish had told me that he and Tom were probably the cleverest boys in the school—potentially anyway. If you decided to swop words with Martin, he said, you needed to be very sure indeed of your ground. So far I had side-stepped all but the most un-ignorable of his transgressions, but I was always uneasily conscious of his heavy, negative presence in the group.

This morning the problem arose over his bedroom, which happened to be the nearest one to my flat on the first floor. After leaving Anthony in the yard, I hurried round the house checking the other jobs, glancing into bedrooms as I passed to make sure they were reasonably tidy. By the time the boys started lining up by the steps for assembly, everything seemed to be in order. A swift count revealed that only Dennis and Desmond were missing from the yard, but I soon located them in the games room, where they were laboriously occupied in filling out a form of some kind in a magazine.

"Come on, you two," I said, "you're the last ones out. Get a move on!"

"But. . ." Dennis waved the magazine.

"Take it with you! Go on—off you go!"

As the two boys flapped out, I remembered that I hadn't checked the two end rooms on the middle corridor. One was Dennis' and Desmond's room, the other was Martin Jarrold's. I hurried up the back stairs, knowing that if I took too long, the queue by the steps would degenerate into a noisy mob. I didn't want to leave it until after assembly because if one of the rooms was in a mess, I would have to face the formidable Mrs. Gage in rascible mood again. I hadn't yet worked out a way to cope with that lady.

The room occupied by Dennis and Desmond was just as it always was, in the sort of nearly-ordered state that is the product of willing incompetence. Dennis always tried hard, and Mrs. Gage had a soft spot for the earnest little boy, so that was alright. I moved along the corridor, intending to cast a very quick glance over the other room, but when I reached the open doorway and looked into Martin's room, I could only stop and stare. My heart sank. The room looked as if an elephant had had an epileptic fit in it. Bedclothes were all over the floor, the mattress was hanging heavily over the side of the bed, drawers were pulled out and their contents strewn around the room, and one curtain had been pulled off its hooks at the end of the rail so that it hung limply and unevenly over the radiator. I took a step forward and then stopped. There was no way I could do a quick tidy-up job on a disaster area like this. I would have to get Martin back to do it. He'd have to miss assembly. If he got into trouble because of that—well, he only had himself to blame. I flew down the main stairs, along the bottom corridor, and out into the yard. The New House boys were lined up by the steps as well now. They neither moved nor spoke as they waited for Steve Hepton, standing on the steps facing them like an effete sergeant-major, to give the signal to move forward into the classroom block. The Old House boys were standing in clumps rather than in a line, laughing and chatting loudly. Henry was giving a chinese burn to a small, very energetic boy called Ronald, whom I'd not had much to do with so far. Ronald was screeching uninhibitedly as the pain in his wrist increased.

"Right!" I shouted, feeling the flush come to my cheeks as I sensed rather than saw Hepton's sardonic smile. "Line up and be quiet! Henry, will you please let go of Ronald's wrist? Now, please!"

"He was cheeky to me, sir," said Henry indignantly. "He called me a bumhole!"

"I don't care what he. . ."

"I did not call him that, sir! I called 'im. . ."

"I'm not interested in what you called him, Ronald. I just want. . ."

"He did call me that, sir! Well—it wasn't quite that. I changed it so it wasn't so rude, sir, but he did call me. . ."

"Well, you're always callin' me names!"

"Look! I've asked you to. . ."

"Well, that's because you're always annoying me—titch!"

"Bumhole!"

"Dolly legs!"

"Bastard!"

"WILL YOU SHUT UP!" I bawled, mortified by the contrast between the behaviour of the two houses.

Why on earth didn't Hepton just wheel his little soldiers in and leave me to get on with it? I knew he was enjoying my discomfiture. Henry and Ronald had postponed hostilities after my final blast, and a straggly but identifiable line had formed. Martin Jarrold was near the back of the queue, towering over Dennis and Desmond who were standing as stiffly to attention as their unsymmetrical shapes would allow. Martin looked bored and apathetic. A lock of black greasy hair hung, as usual, over his eyes.

"Martin," I called, from the front of the line, "I think you know what I'm about to say to you."

Total silence fell immediately. Confrontation between myself and Martin was potentially high entertainment as far as the rest of the boys were concerned.

"Yes, sir," said Martin unexpectedly, pushing the hair from his eyes.

I blinked. Surely it wasn't going to be that easy!

"Well, will you just go and do it then, please, Martin."

"Yes, sir," said Martin, "I will."

I was so taken aback by the cooperative nature of the boy's response that it hardly registered for a moment or two that, after slouching away from his place in the line, he was heading, not towards the house, but the opposite way in the direction of the back of the classroom block where the 'invisible' smoking bush was situated.

"Where are you going, Martin?" I enquired bewilderedly.

He stopped, turning his gaze on me with heavy patience.

"I'm going to go and do it, like you said, sir."

"Do what?"

"Have a fag, sir."

"Have a. . ?"

"Yes, sir. You said you thought I knew what you were about to say to me. I did. I knew you were about to say you wanted me to go and have a fag. Then you told me to go and do it, so I'm just going round the back to have one. Something wrong?"

There was a chorus of delighted laughter from Old and New House boys. Behind me I could hear Steve Hepton joining in quietly. I took a deep breath. Would I ever be able to face this kind of situation without shaking so stupidly?

"Go and wait for me outside the Old House office, Martin," I said through my teeth.

"I've only got one fag I'm afraid, sir, if that's what you're hoping. Still, we could share it if you like."

Another burst of laughter erupted from Martin's ecstatic audience as the tall figure turned and sauntered nonchalantly towards the Old House. Hepton tapped me on the shoulder.

"Hope you don't think I'm interfering, old chap," he whispered, "but why don't I take both lots in while you go and do a bit of the old miracle-working with our humorous friend?"

It was too good an offer to refuse, whatever I thought of the way in which it was couched. As I walked across the yard, I heard the New House housemaster address my boys.

"Right, you lot! Cabaret's over. You're not dealing with the soft brigade now."

To my intense chagrin, the laughter and comments were instantly checked. What was it that he'd got, for goodness sake?

Back in the house I found Martin Jarrold draped over the big radiator near the foot of the main stairs. I decided to be completely straight-forward this time.

"Your room's a mess," I said bluntly. "I want you to go and clear it up."

"And I want you to go and clear it up," said Martin easily, "so we'll toss a coin, shall we?"

I passed the tip of my tongue over uncomfortably dry lips.

"I don't see why you should get away with doing—I mean not doing things that everyone else doesn't get away with doing - not doing, I mean. . ."

I stopped speaking. I'd got completely muddled. My tongue felt enormous.

'You know what I mean," I said hoarsely.

"Well I'm glad I do," he sneered, "because you obviously don't."

"Now, look!"

"I don't see anything worth looking at," drawled the boy.

He dragged himself off the radiator and stretched luxuriously.

"Think I'll go and have that fag after all. There's nothing worth staying here for. Don't forget to get my room done, Harper. I'll check it later—or I might get Mr. Hepton to check it. He knows what's what."

This last remark was accompanied by a loose-lipped leer of pure malice. He turned, hands in his pockets, and started to stroll along the corridor.

I knew I was either going to burst into tears or hit him.

I caught him up, spun him round by the shoulders and smacked him once, very hard on the face, with the flat of my right hand. I knew a bare instant of total satisfaction as the blow landed, and a world of remorse and shame immediately afterwards, especially when I witnessed the reaction to what I'd done. This big awkward boy wasn't a tough guy at all. My smack sent him cowering back against the wall, covering his face with his hands and producing little shrieking gasps as though he feared that more blows were about to follow. His total disintegration threw me completely. It just didn't seem possible that someone could move from casual, sneering confidence to abject terror in such a short time.

There was a great coldness inside me. I had struck a boy. My career as a residential worker was over. I left Martin, still crouched against the wall, and went upstairs to my flat.

It was a relief to close the door behind me, but as soon as I walked into the living room I was confronted by the wreckage of last night, and the emotional echoes of Tom's anguish. The only place left was my bedroom. As soon as I was in there with the door safely closed, I dragged all my shoes from the bottom of the wardrobe, climbed in, and pulled the door shut. I was hidden from them all in the enfolding darkness. No one could threaten me with a knife, or destroy my dignity, or make me feel useless, or even sack me, because they didn't know where I was. Sitting in my coffin-like retreat, I pictured what must be happening now. Martin would have gone directly to Mr. Rowley, or George Ashton perhaps, and reported that I had attacked him. They would have sat him down with paper and pen, I guessed, to record the incident in detail, then, after a solemn discussion, it would be decided that I had to go. The next stage in the proceedings would be Mrs. Philips arriving at my door, sadly but dutifully announcing that the headmaster wanted to see me immediately in his office, and that would be that. So real was this scenario in my imagination, that when the doorbell rang a minute later, I automatically assumed that it must be the school secretary waiting outside. It did occur to me that the whole process had happened rather speedily, but then, I reflected gloomily, it was an open and shut case really. The question was—should I open the door or not. I waited. There was quite a long pause, then the bell went again.

"What the hell!" I said to myself. "Let's get it over with." Easing my concertinaed body out of the wardrobe, I opened the bedroom door and stood in the little hall space for a moment trying to compose myself for the coming ordeal. I opened the door.

"Alright Mrs. Philips, I know. . . ."

"I've done my room, sir."

It was Martin. Not cowering now, but certainly not wearing the lazily arrogant expression that he usually adopted when speaking to me.

"Do you want to check it, sir?"

I followed him along the corridor and into his bedroom. The transformation was startling. Everything was back where it should be. I nodded in a dazed way.

"Yes—yes, Martin, it's fine, but. . ?"

"Yes, sir?"

"Martin, I don't want you to do things because I hit you. I hated myself after I'd hit you. I'm not the sort of person who - I don't think I'm the sort of person who hits people. . ."

"It wasn't because you hit me, it was because you didn't."

"I didn't?"

"I was brought up by my uncle, sir. He was a big, tall, fat man, and he wasn't very interested in me. So I used to say things to wind him up. I got very good at it. I didn't mind him getting angry because it meant he took notice of me. But—sometimes - he'd go right over the top and really lay into me. I thought you were going to downstairs—but you didn't. I can't stand it if someone hits me. I turn into a jelly-baby."

I scratched my head and stared helplessly at this sixteen year old talking so calmly and with such insight about himself and his past.

"I still want to apologise for hitting you, Martin," I persisted.

"I had no right to do that. Only—if I say that, are you going to assume I'm weak and go back to making me look foolish in front of everyone again?"

A look of real amusement appeared in the dark, intelligent eyes.

"You're a funny member of staff, you are, sir. A sort of cross between Mike Merry and Mr. Parish."

The friendly tone in the boy's voice robbed the words of any offence.

"Well, the thing is, Martin, that you would almost certainly win any battle of words. I've got this uneasy feeling that you're brighter than me. I'll promise to do anything I can for you, if you promise to only unleash fifty per cent of your intelligence on me at any one time."

He pushed his bottom lip out and blew upwards to dislodge the hair from its familiar position over his eyes.

"Okay, sir." Then suddenly embarrassed, "I'd better be getting to school, sir."

I stood in the corridor for a moment, listening to Martin clumping down stairs. I'd had two dramatic confrontations that morning. One with Anthony, and another with Martin. A third, perhaps, with myself. I had been both the near-victim of violence, and also its agent. I had thought the sack was imminent because I had struck someone, and instead, things had worked out much better than I could have hoped because I hadn't struck him more. I had learned something—sensed a strange power in honesty when I was talking just now. I doubted very much that this morning's episode with Anthony would have made any significant impact, but I knew somehow that something real had happened in these last few moments with Martin.

Chapter Twelve

"Apart from breaking just about every rule in the book, David, you've done very well."

The headmaster was seated comfortably on his office carpet, back against the wall, legs stretched out straight in front of him, eyes peacefully closed as they had been ever since I started to describe my dealings with the boys over the last few days.

"What do you mean?" I asked, a little perturbed. Had I really broken 'just about every rule?' What were the rules?

It was nearly lunchtime. After my first DIY lesson with George Ashton (the recalcitrant locker door had flown into position as soon as the deputy headmaster looked at it), I had been summoned to Mr. Rowley's office for the second of what I now knew were termed 'supervision sessions'. On my way over to the office block, I asked myself whether I was going to mention that I had struck Martin Jarrold or not.

"No," I replied firmly to myself, "I am not! The incident is over and done with. It's not worth bringing it up. It could do more harm than good. I'll just forget about it."

And yet, once I had relaxed and got into the swing of talking about events and people and the way they had made me feel, it all came out quite naturally—not just the things that might show me in a good light, but everything else as well. My lack of judgement with Anthony, my feeling of helplessness with Tom on top of the Peak, even the fact that I had sat in the bottom of my wardrobe after committing the cardinal sin of striking Martin. The headmaster was so still and so unheadmasterish, sitting there on the floor with his feet sticking out, that all my inhibitions seemed to disappear. Now, as I waited for Mr. Rowley to explain what he meant, I wondered if I should have been more careful.

"For instance," he said, "you became emotionally entangled with Tom's problem. You failed to remain detached from your client. You wept when he wept. A major mistake. Any expert in child care will tell you that personal involvement is undesirable to say the least."

Mr. Rowley still hadn't opened his eyes. I didn't know what to say.

"But I was only. . ."

"In addition there was your honesty with Martin after you had smacked him. Good residential workers cash in on advantages. They do not risk destroying them by indulging in the pleasure of speaking from the heart. And then, of course, there was the blow itself, a lesser crime than involvement naturally, but nevertheless a form of punishment that is expressly forbidden by County Council rules."

The last phrase rang a bell.

"Like smoking, you mean?"

Mr. Rowley opened his eyes and smiled crookedly at me.

"Precisely, David. Just like smoking. All through what I risibly describe as my professional life, I have wasted more time and energy on the smoking problem than on almost anything else. There appears to be a pleasure in the oral satisfaction of smoking that is unparalleled by any other activity—at least, as far as many of the children I have worked with are concerned. I have known more stealing and wheeling and dealing and bullying and lying over cigarettes, than any other single issue in all the residential establishments that I have been involved with. Especially, I might add, in those establishments where it is forbidden altogether. For years I upheld other people's regimes, dutifully pursuing and punishing and decrying the habit with appropriate evangelical fervour. Occasionally I paused to wonder why so much effort had not only a minimal effect, but actually seemed to provoke more problems than it solved."

"So the bush. . ?"

"The bush—the nonexistent bush—is a kind of answer to the problem. When I finally left the approved school system and was offered the opportunity to become headmaster of a brand new boarding school here at Stapley, I determined that I would not allow life to be dominated by problems associated with cigarettes. I decided to nominate a small area in the grounds which would be neither visited nor 'noticed' by staff, where boys can safely smoke. I have never formally announced this fact, I have 'leaked' it. I have also made quite sure that all boys are aware that in the event of this arrangement being abused, I shall proceed to 'notice' the bush for as long as is necessary. So far. . .''

He rubbed the patches of hair on the sides of his head until they looked like two over-used pan scourers.

"So far it has worked, I am very pleased to say."

"But you're not saying the same about members of staff hitting the children, are you? You're not saying we have to accept it and—well—let it happen, surely?''

He shook his head.

"Of course not, David. I have no intention of running a school where children are physically ill-treated, and I do my very best to avoid employing people who revert to such methods of control.''

I looked down at my hands resting in my lap.

"What about me? I hit Martin this morning. . .''

"Yes," interrupted the headmaster, "and you nearly died of guilt and worry afterwards. What's more—you told me about it. I don't somehow see you as an agent of brutality, David. What happened this morning is a learning experience for you, and for Martin by the sound of it. You must have utterly confused him by being so open and honest afterwards. That was absolutely perfect—absolutely right.''

I looked up, puzzled.

"But just now you said. . .''

He waved an apologetic hand.

"Forgive me, David. I am diseased with irony. It is a serious fault. I do strongly believe in being quite honest with children, and as for getting personally or emotionally involved, well. . . they have a point, of course, those who say that it is never a good idea, but I have seen so many children in my time who suffer the same fate as the county car.''

"What do you mean?''

Mr. Rowley drew his legs up and folded his arms round his knees.

"In almost every residential children's establishment you will find one or more vehicles supplied by the local authority for the purpose of transporting children. These cars are for general use. They belong to everybody, and therefore to nobody. They are frequently left unlocked, and seldom cleaned. They are usually parked fairly carelessly, and minor collisions with walls or gates or posts are not regarded as matters of great importance since the repair bill is footed by the county. Every now and then they are removed for statutory servicing by experts whose interest is purely commercial. Eventually, after a brief but eventful career involving a great deal of misuse, they are auctioned off to people who subsequently ask themselves who could possibly have owned a vehicle that has so patently lacked the special care and attention that the majority of private cars receive. They were never special to anybody. . ."

He was staring into the distance as he spoke. Now he turned his head and looked straight through at me, the lines of a familiar pain scoring his forehead and the corners of his eyes.

"So many children, David. . . so many, many children."

He sighed.

"In some ways, David, I am the worst possible person to advise and supervise you. I cannot rule out emotional attachment in my own work with the boys. Indeed, in some cases it is only a bond of that kind that can offer hope for the future, or at the very least, a vague memory in later life of being valued and liked by 'that bloke at that school I went to.' Mark Parish now, he would be able to offer you the best possible advice on how to approach work from the other angle. He is the most effective exponent I know of non-attached, but consistently positive, work with children. Some of us, though, have got to get involved in a different way, painful and disappointing though that may be at times. However—on to other matters. . ."

The headmaster leaned over on one hand and pushed himself back up onto his feet.

"I hear you are contemplating a camping expedition."

"Errr. . . yes, I was thinking I might go with my fiancee, Annie. . ."

Damn and blast my blushing!

Mr. Rowley was settled in his desk chair now, an amused little smile pulling at his mouth.

"Does she drive, David?"

"No, Mr. Rowley, she doesn't. I hadn't thought of that actually. We'd need a driver, wouldn't we? Especially if we needed to err. . . drive anywhere."

"Quite," said the headmaster gravely. He tapped the desk top in a brisk rhythm with the end of his pen. "I rather think, in any case, that you would be well-advised to ask someone with a little more experience to accompany you for your first camp. Mr. Merry is a keen camper, and very amiable company. Why not ask him if he would be interested?"

A wave of relief passed through me. What a good idea! Having Mike on an expedition of that kind would make it just right.

"Yes," I nodded, "I'll do that—thank you." I got up to go. "Oh, by the way, Mr. Rowley, I did just want to ask you about files. I know that each boy's got a set of records, but I wondered who has access to them. Can I see them?"

Mr. Rowley gestured expansively.

"Help yourself, David. They're all in Doreen's office in the tall grey filing cabinet. Read them by all means. I hesitated to direct you towards them when you first came, because I wanted you to judge the accuracy of the file by comparing it with the boy you know, rather than the other way round. You may recall that in our last meeting I suggested that our boys are, as it were, trapped in a hall of distorting mirrors. Each mirror—family, friends, school, staff—throws back a different reflection. The file is a very dangerous mirror for disturbed children. They know it is there, but they are not allowed to see it. They fear it because it may be inaccurate, and sometimes because it tells the truth. Tom would dearly love to burn his file. I would like to lend him the matches, but I have my own responsibilities, just as you do."

Mr. Rowley smiled warmly at me as I stood uncertainly at the door.

"Have a good camp at the weekend, David. I'm sure you will."

By lunchtime that day the camp was more or less organised. I managed to grab Mike Merry at twelve-thirty and, after a quick phone call to his wife, he confirmed that he would be more than happy to join us, especially as we would only be staying away for one night. In a letter to Annie I told her about the plan for the weekend and said how much I'd like her to come, adding - completely dishonestly—that I would understand if it didn't appeal to her. Ruth agreed to prepare menus and pack food, which left Mike and I to sort out and get together camping equipment from the store over by the football pitch. That could be done during the next couple of days. I found it all rather exciting.

I decided that, in addition to whichever boys were left at the weekend in the Old House, I would also ask Howard and Tom if they'd like to join us. This I did, having gritted my teeth and checked with Steve Hepton first. Howard's response was immediate and enthusiastic.

"Cor, yeah! I'll come! Fanks, sir!"

Tom's response was quite different. He was in my flat, handing things to George Ashton as he mended my windows, when I asked him.

"Thank you for asking me, sir," he said, "but I've asked JD—my brother Justin—over for Saturday, and he's said he'll come."

Tom looked surprised and excited when he said this. I felt pleased for him. Something new happening.

"Never mind, Tom," I said cheerfully, "that's far more important. Next time perhaps, eh?"

"Oh yes, sir," said Tom, "I'll certainly come next time."

That afternoon I walked down into Stapley village and, for the first time since the day of my interview, followed the wooden sign down between the thatched cottages and across the green to the church. Inside, the daffodils were gone, and there was no shaft of sunlight pouring through the tinted window. The whole atmosphere in the little church was more grey, more solid—more real. But the answer to the question I had asked on that first day was still 'Yes'. The only difference was in my acceptance and understanding of that 'Yes'. It was more gritty, more solid and much more real.

Chapter Thirteen

"Cor, sir! Innit excitin', sir!"

We were on our way to camp, and Dennis was ecstatic. I twisted round in the front passenger seat of the old green school van, and looked at the mass of bodies, food, camping equipment and spare clothing that was jammed into every available space. Six tents, twelve sleeping bags (one spare in case 'someone' had an accident), one toilet tent, one store tent, five primus stoves, eleven sets of mugs, plates and eating irons, three large cardboard boxes, each containing provisions of various kinds, and, poked into corners and shoved into gaps, all the other bits and pieces that had seemed so vitally important when we were planning our expedition.

"Are we nearly there, sir?"

We had been travelling for only twenty minutes, and it was the third time Dennis had asked the same question.

"No, Dennis," I smiled, "we've got quite a way to go yet. Why don't you play a game with Desmond for a while. If you breathe on the window you can play noughts and crosses with your fingers."

Desmond, packed strategically between Dennis and a pile of tents, nodded happily.

"Thank you, sir," he creaked, "for a good suggestion. We will do it!"

Somehow the two boys managed to squeeze their bodies round so that they were both facing the glass. They began to breathe loudly and hoarsely in the direction of the window. The game might hold their attention for a minute or two.

Both Dennis and Desmond were wildly excited about the prospect of camping, although Dennis had never actually slept in a tent before. Desmond, on the other hand, claimed to have extensive experience of the activity and had greatly impressed Dennis over the last few days with his suave references to tent pegs and latrines and primuses. He was to be in charge of their tent pitching and cooking activities, while Dennis occupied the humble role of apprentice and labourer. Privately I had severe doubts about Desmond's self-advertised expertise, but with a careful eye kept on him, I was sure he'd manage reasonably well. My most immediate problem as far as Desmond was concerned was his bowel control. If he should have an accident now, as we travelled along in the van, the result would be unthinkable. In such a confined space there would be no escape. I prayed that he would stay calm.

Opposite Dennis and Desmond sat Anthony, who had been quite unexcited about the whole business until he happened to wander into the kitchen as Ruth was packing the food away in boxes. The sight of piles of bacon, cartons of eggs, and tins of cake, turned him into a camper on the spot. He sat quietly now, his eyes occasionally twitching towards the cardboard containers, knowing that if you waited long enough, lunchtime always came. Anthony still made me feel uneasy. I hated to see anything sharp in or near his hands. If only there was something about him that I could really like. It would make things so much easier. . .

"Alright, sir?"

Howard, sitting on the far side of Anthony, had looked up from the comic he was reading and caught my eye. Dazzled as usual by the brilliance of his smile, I nodded and smiled back.

"Yes, I'm fine thanks, Twinkle. Looking forward to it?"

"Yessir," he replied, "'sgonna be a larf. I'll dig the 'oles for the toilet stuff when we get there, sir. Zat alright?"

"Great!" I said. "Thanks."

Howard went back to his comic. I knew why he'd said that about digging disposal holes for the chemical toilet when we arrived. Earlier, he had nearly lost his place on the camp because of yet another temper. It had happened shortly before we set off that Saturday morning. Howard, who had all week seemed genuinely pleased and keen on the idea of joining us for the one-night camp, had been told by Ruth Crompton that he would be sharing a tent with Anthony. After going away and brooding over this for a few minutes he had appeared in the New House dining room and started to throw furniture around as one of his famous rages mounted towards its peak. Mrs. Murchison, hearing the noise from the kitchen and being the only adult in the vicinity, had very wisely decided not to tackle him. Instead, she sent one of the boys who was helping in the kitchen to find Mrs. Crompton or Mr. Ashton, and another into the Old House to fetch whoever was on duty there. I was busily strapping down a large rucksack in my flat at the time, so it was a while before I was located and summoned to the scene. I don't mind admitting that I was enormously relieved on crashing through the swing doors into the New House, to find that George Ashton had got there before me. Unlike Mike Merry on the previous occasion, George seemed to have a very secure grip on the struggling boy, but the language was just the same. He'd been effing well looking forward to this effing camp, and now he had to share a tent with that effing great fat blank, and what sort of effing fun was that going to be, for eff's sake! We, the staff, were all a load of effing blanks, and he wouldn't go on the effing camp if we effing well paid him so why didn't we all eff off and leave him alone?

In the midst of this tirade, Tom walked in and, seeing what was happening, stopped and waited quietly by the door.

George Ashton didn't try any distraction ploys as the headmaster had done, but he did do something that proved to have an even more lasting effect. He had been holding the boy from behind with one arm in a half-nelson, and the other wrapped around his neck. Suddenly he spun him round, caught hold of both his wrists, and shouted straight into his face from a few inches away. His voice contained a strange mixture of entreaty, anger and excitement.

"This is it, son! This is a bad temper—you're right in the middle of a bad temper! This is when you can *do* something about it—this is when you can say 'I *don't* have to give in to my temper!' You can do it, son—you can do it *now*! Fight it! Go on—fight it right now!"

Howard looked like someone frozen in the middle of a fit. Lips drawn back over his gums, eyes crazy with anger, he was suspended for a moment, then words spilt through his teeth.

"Anyway—who cares?"

"I DO!" blasted George. "Don't do it—don't give in! You don't want to have tempers like this, so don't! Stop now, please, son—do it! Control yourself because you want to, damn you! It'll change your life! Do you understand?''

"Go on, Twinkle," said Tom's quiet voice from the door. "See if you can."

That seemed to tip the balance. Howard's head jerked round abruptly when Tom spoke, then back again as George said just one more word.

"Well?"

A great battle was fought and won in the next moment. Howard suddenly relaxed physically, and an expression of puzzlement and relief crept over his boxer's features. When he spoke, his voice was surprisingly even and strong.

"Can I go an' finish packin', please, sir?"

George released his wrists and the boy headed for the door. Stopping in the doorway, he turned and spoke once more.

"Fanks, sir. I'll come an' put all the chairs an' stuff straight in a mo'.''

"Yes," I thought, watching the tousled head bounce with the rhythm of the van as Howard lost himself again in his comic, "it may have been a great moment, but he'll still feel the need to pay for his temper with a spot of latrine digging!"

In the rear section of the van sat Annie, surrounded by the four leading members of her new fan club. There was no doubt that as far as Henry, Robert, Arnold and Colin were concerned, she had scored an enormous hit. Watching her now, chatting so easily and unselfconsciously to the little group of boys, I felt a mixture of jealousy and pride. Jealousy, because she related so freely and honestly to them. She had a natural dignity and strength that didn't need to be constantly reinforced by shouting or physical strength. I had wanted to impress her, but already she had made a more real contact with these boys than I felt I was capable of.

Perhaps I didn't want her to come and work with me after all.

But then, as well as all these ignoble feelings, I was proud of her. So calm and beautiful and intelligent, and—perhaps most important of all in the circumstances—she had made an immediate and devoted slave out of Colin. I had been rather nervous about Colin's inclusion in the party, but the combination of Douglas' absence and Annie's presence seemed to have produced a less aggressive, more playful personality than the one I was accustomed to. I looked at him now seated next to Annie, demonstrating obscure knots with a piece of nylon rope, his face civilised by the pleasure of imparting knowledge. Her expression was one of rapt attention. She looked as though all she wanted out of life was to know how to tie obscure knots in pieces of nylon rope. Yes, from the point of view of Colin. . .

"Are we there yet, sir?"

"If you ask that one more time, Dennis," called Mike Merry from the driver's seat, "I shall stop the van, come back there, and throttle you with one of your own socks."

"You won't need to frottle 'im wiv it, sir," called back Howard, momentarily roused from his comic, "just 'old it near 'is nose an' 'e'll suffocate."

There was a chorus of laughter from the back of the van, but it was good-natured laughter. Only Desmond looked a little uneasy. Jokes about smells were dangerous. Overall, there was a good atmosphere in the van. I turned to face the front again. I was looking forward to this camp.

The campsite turned out to be ideal. Owned by the Forestry Commission, it was situated on a wide grassy bank of the river Blay, a very fast moving current, flowing at this stage of its seaward journey between high, steep banks planted out with firs by the Commission. The site was nearly a mile from the nearest public road and connected to the opposite bank of the river only by a long metal pedestrian suspension bridge which, we soon discovered, shook and rattled loudly whenever anyone used it to cross over.

The only other tent on the site was a small two-man ridge tent, pitched quite close to the river. As we drove the van off the rough track onto the grass, I caught a glimpse of a face watching us from the door flap.

It took nearly two hours to erect the seven tents in a rough circle with the door flaps facing inward towards the spot where we intended to light our fire. Mike Merry, who was the least impractical of us, moved from tent to tent advising and assisting, but the bulk of his time was spent with Desmond and Dennis. At first, Desmond had politely refused assistance, the gist of his remarks being that Mike's time would be better spent with the novices than with a veteran camper such as himself. He then set about instructing Dennis in a loud military sort of voice, issuing a set of commands so confusing that Dennis ended up rushing frantically around, poking pegs indiscriminately into anything that remotely resembled a loop. The result was a strange, slab-like affair, no more than three inches high at any one point. Having run out of pegs at last, Dennis rose to his feet and looked enquiringly at his instructor.

"Not much room in there, Desmond," he said worriedly. "Did I do somethin' wrong?"

My tent was the next one to theirs. I laid my handful of pegs down for a moment and called to Desmond.

"How about getting Mike Merry to have a quick look at it, Desmond? You and Dennis have done a great job, but he might have some ideas about how to make it even better."

"My goodness, darling," whispered Annie, temporarily redundant since Colin had insisted on putting her tent up for her. "You're such a diplomat! I wish you'd take all that trouble to avoid hurting my feelings."

"I get paid for not hurting their feelings," I whispered back. "But I'm sure we could come to some arrangement. Say—a pound for each kind word?"

"I'll think about it," said Annie, nodding very solemnly. "It could be worth it."

Desmond had clearly reached a decision about my suggestion.

"You might be right, sir," he said in his slow, creaky voice. "I think I'll ask Mr. Merry for some advice."

Dennis was despatched to summon Mike, who was swatting Anthony away from the food boxes as one might swat a fat wasp. I winked at the genial teacher as he arrived on the scene of Dennis' efforts.

"Desmond and I were just wondering if there were any finishing touches you'd recommend for this tent, Mr. Merry. Any little improvements or changes. . ."

Mike walked slowly round the flat, un-tent-like object which Dennis had pinned securely to the ground. When he got back to the place where he'd started, he turned to address Desmond and Dennis in casually impartial tones.

"Well," he said, stroking his beard thoughtfully, "there is a school of thought that says one should use tent poles in the construction of the tent."

He bent down and picked up a long, orange bag that rattled and clanked as soon as he touched it.

"I can see that you go along with those who claim that you don't need tent poles," went on Mike, "only they do have their uses, you know."

Desmond turned to Dennis.

"They do have their uses, you know, Dennis," he said sternly, as though Dennis had flatly refused to use tent poles in his first attempt.

Dennis looked crestfallen.

"Isn't it no good then, sir?"

"It's extremely good!" said Mike, clapping a hand on the little boy's shoulder. "It's just that Desmond here isn't aware of some of the new ideas that are around. Tell you what—why don't I show you how to use the poles properly, and you tell me if you think I'm doing anything wrong?"

Desmond and Dennis nodded and beamed.

"Right! Dennis, you start pulling the pegs out, and Desmond can take the poles out of the bag and lay them on the ground. . ."

"Right!" said Desmond, reverting to his military style of command.

"You start pulling the pegs out, Private Dennis, and I'll take the poles out of the bag and lay them on the ground. . ."

By early evening everything was more or less shipshape. Our little ring of 'A' shaped tents looked quite cosy and inviting in the flickering light of the camp fire which Robert had offered to build and light. He was good at it too, and deliriously happy in an environment which allowed him to be as dirty and untidy as even he could possibly wish.

The wood collection had been allocated to a group of five. Annie, myself, Colin and Arnold—who were sharing a tent—and Anthony, who, it was felt, had not contributed sufficiently to the work that Howard had put in on getting their tent up. Anthony mumbled a little at this, but supper was not yet a reality and he'd been told there was none for him if he didn't collect wood, so he rolled along behind us picking up the occasional small stick, grunting heavily each time as if it was a tremendous effort.

Colin, on the other hand, was definitely out to impress. He strode ahead as we penetrated the woods which began at the base of the sharply rising valley side, picking up logs with as much careless ease as he could manage, until he was almost tottering under the weight of wood in his arms. Annie, the person for whom the whole manly performance was intended, produced frequent gasps and little cries of admiration, until a point not very far into the belt of trees where it became obvious that Colin would collapse if so much as a leaf was added to his load. She called out to him.

"Colin, my love, why don't you take that pile back and then come and get some more? You really have done well! I don't know how you can manage to carry so much."

Purple with effort, Colin spoke in short, jerky sentences as he fought to conceal his breathlessness.

"'Seasy, miss. Not heavy really. G'back. Gessomore. . ."

He staggered back down the path towards the campsite. Nothing was going to make him drop that wood while we could still see him. Anthony, who he passed on the way, looked disbelievingly from Colin's heavy burden to the few spindly bits clutched in his own fist, then bent thoughtfully to pick up another little twig to add to his collection.

Arnold had been walking quietly beside us all this time, filling a plastic carrier bag with pieces of bark and medium sized kindling. Now he suggested we should sit on the trunk of a fallen tree and wait for Colin. Somehow he managed to insert himself between Annie and I just as I thought I was sitting next to her. There was a strange little smile on his face as he gazed down the slope to where he could see Anthony peering hopefully at something that might have been a dried up chestnut from last year, and further on, Colin's wavering figure about to disappear from sight round a bend in the path. Annie had noticed the expression on Arnold's face as well.

"What are you thinking about, Arnold?" she asked quietly.

"I was pretending, miss," said Arnold dreamily.

"Call me Annie."

Arnold blushed.

"What are you pretending, Arnold?" she persisted.

I suddenly knew who Arnold reminded me of. Years ago, as a child, I had listened to the Archie Andrews show on the radio every Sunday. Archie Andrews was a ventriloquist's dummy, a perpetual schoolboy made of something other than flesh and blood. Sometimes he appeared on television with his operator, Peter Brough.

Archie was an archetypal schoolboy, square-jawed but immature, with a voice that had only just broken. I remembered thinking that he was funny and clever, but pathetic. He would never be able to grow up because he was made of wood. He was rather like Arnold.

"I was pretending," said Arnold, "that I was sitting here resting in the middle of a walk with my mother and father. I was pretending that you and Mr. Harper were my parents, and we'd decided to go for a stroll in the wood near our house before we all sat down to have dinner together, and later on, when we got home, you'd both ask me how school was going, and you'd look really interested when I talked about maths even if you didn't understand the problems, but you'd pretend you did because you wanted to encourage me, and then, when I'd watched some TV I'd go to bed and Mr. Harper would tuck me in like he does at school, and you'd. . ."

"Yes?" said Annie as Arnold paused. Her eyes were swimming with unshed tears.

Arnold's voice was very low and subdued as he went on.

"You'd kiss me goodnight and say 'I love you, Arnold, and I'm very proud of you,' and I'd go to sleep feeling. . . okay."

The boy's head dropped in embarrassment. Annie shook her head at me in silent desperation across his bowed shoulders. I knew what she was thinking. What could you say? What could you do? We weren't his parents. We couldn't do those things for him—at least, not in the special, exclusive way that he needed.

Later, when all the wood had been collected, and we were trudging back down the path behind the boys, Annie looked at me over her armful of kindling.

"Do you really tuck Arnold in at night, David?" she asked.

"Yes," I said, colouring slightly, "I do. I felt a little bit embarrassed about it at first, but it's just something I do now. Why?"

"I'm going to kiss you when I get a chance," said Annie inexplicably.

Our evening meal around the fire that evening was a memorable experience. Mike Merry, who was a very able open-air chef, took pity on us all and produced the whole thing single handed. As usual, the tin plateful of sausage, bacon, eggs and fried bread tasted like something not of this earth, and the very ordinary tinned rice, taken from very ordinary tins, lived up to its brand name for once. Afterwards, when the washing up had been done, and Mike had taken most of the group off for a torchlight exploration of the area, we were joined by the two occupants of the little tent we had noticed when we first arrived. They were lads of fifteen or sixteen, naturally shy, but also very anxious looking. They sat side by side on a log beside the fire and explained that they had a problem.

"Last night some blokes from the caravan site up on the other side of the valley came over the bridge and really scared us," said the larger of the two, an earnest, well spoken boy with sculpted hair and very white teeth.

"What did they actually do?" asked Annie.

"You shoulda smacked their 'eads in for 'em," broke in Colin, glowing aggressively in the firelight.

"We couldn't do anything," said the boy. "There must have been about seven or eight of them, and they stood in a circle round the tent, not letting us get out and saying they were going to throw the whole thing into the river with us in it."

"An' they cut our tent," put in the smaller boy, his voice wavering a little as he recalled the fear he had felt. "There's a big slit in the fly-sheet where one of them just ripped it with his knife. It's a new one too," he added pathetically.

"Anyway," continued the other, "they went away in the end, but they said they were going to come back tonight and attack us with axes and iron bars while we're asleep in the tent. We were going to pack up and go today, but when we saw you arriving in your van, we thought we'd stay and see if you could help us."

Colin picked a stick up from the grass near his feet and bashed it against the log he was sitting on so that it snapped loudly.

"Mr. 'Arper'll gettem for yer!" he snarled confidently. Then turning to me, "Won't yer, sir?"

"Don't worry, boys," said Annie calmly, but with equal confidence, "this gentlemen sleeps in that tent over there,"—she pointed—"so if you have any problems tonight, don't hesitate to wake him up and he'll come and sort the whole thing out for you, won't you, David?"

In the comforting light from the fire, and while the situation was still a hypothetical one, and with Colin and Annie watching me from either side waiting for me to confirm their trust in my heroic intentions and abilities, it all seemed so easy somehow. Colin and Annie believed in me. It felt good. I nodded reassuringly.

"Relax, lads, we'll handle anything that crops up. Just give me a call and I'll be there in a matter of seconds. Okay?"

The two boys went back to their tent a few minutes later in a much happier frame of mind. They were chattering and laughing as they passed into the darkness beyond the range of the light from our fire. For a fleeting moment I felt uneasy about my John Wayne act. Supposing I was called out at two in the morning to confront seven heavily armed psychopaths? I dismissed the notion. Almost certainly nothing would happen.

By the time Mike arrived back with the others it was time for an evening drink. Desmond and Dennis were delighted. They hadn't been allowed to use their primus stove for anything yet. Mike had used the big double burner to prepare the evening meal. Now they were to be given a plastic mug each, containing sugar, milk and cocoa-powder, and left with their primus ready-lit so that all they had to do was pour the liquid from the mugs into a saucepan, heat it up until it was ready to pour back into the mugs, and then simply drink it.

"You're sure you can manage, are you?" said Annie, as she handed them the mugs. "You just heat it up in the saucepan."

"Yes, miss," said Dennis excitedly, spilling a little of the mixture, "Desmond knows about—about, well, drinks an' suchlike."

The expert on 'drinks an' suchlike,' his reputation as an expert camper still intact in Dennis' eyes despite the tent problems, smirked self-consciously.

"I think I can manage a cuppa cocoa, miss," he creaked with a rather unsuccessful attempt at a debonair wink.

"Aren't they sweet," giggled Annie, as the two boys set off in slow motion, balancing their mugs in their hands, towards the spot where the little stove was burning beside their tent.

If the wind had been blowing in a different direction, we might have realised even earlier that something was amiss with Dennis and Desmond's cocoa preparation. Everyone else was settled round the fire cuddling their hot mugs in their hands as the temperature dropped to quite an uncomfortable level, when Henry raised his head and started to sniff the air with a puzzled expression on his face.

"What's that funny smell?" he asked, wrinkling his nose. "What smell?" said Anthony in a muffled voice. He seemed to be trying to get his head into his empty mug so that he could lick the bottom.

"It smells like. . . I dunno what it smells like."

"I can smell it now," exclaimed Mike. "It smells like. . ."

"It's comin' from where Desmond an' Dennis are, sir," said Robert, "but it's not. . . 'that'."

I didn't have to ask Robert what he meant by 'that'. There had already been an occasion since our arrival when Desmond had gone missing and shortly afterwards the toilet tent had developed a life of its own. Annie, with great fortitude, had approached the tall canvas cabinet and asked it why it was trying to strangle itself. A small voice from inside revealed itself as belonging to Desmond, who was desperately trying to cope with one of his 'accidents'. Annie had dealt with the situation very quickly and efficiently, leaving Desmond's self-respect virtually undented.

But it wasn't that kind of smell that was wafting across from Desmond's direction now. It was strong and unpleasant, but it was more like something burning—or melting perhaps. . .

"It's burnin' rubber, sir," said Robert, standing up and pointing to where Dennis and Desmond were still crouched over their primus stove with their backs towards the fire. "They're burnin' some rubber, sir."

"No they're not!" shouted Mike, jumping to his feet as realisation hit him. "They're burning mugs—plastic mugs!"

We all followed Mike over to the increasingly offensive smell, and formed a ring round the two boys, who were studying the phenomenon before them with considerable puzzlement. Inside the saucepan that had been placed on the burning stove, stood the two plastic mugs containing cocoa mixture. A thick, reeking smoke emanated from the point where the pan made contact with the bottom of the mugs. Mike, who had obviously already guessed what was going on, grabbed the saucepan handle, lifted the whole thing off the primus and turned it upside down. The liquid spattered down onto the grass, but the mugs remained where they were. They were melted onto the base of the pan.

Dennis looked at Annie rather mournfully.

"Did we do somethin' wrong again, miss?"

"Well, I really meant that you should pour the cocoa into the saucepan," said Annie gently. "Plastic melts when it gets very hot, you see."

"Didn't you know plastic melts when it gets very hot, Dennis?" said Desmond frowningly. "It does, you know."

"Come on, you two," grinned Mike. "I'll make you a drink on our stove. What d'you fancy—rubber flavour, plastic flavour, or just plain cocoa flavour?"

I must have been asleep for about half an hour in the tent I was sharing with Mike Merry, when I realised that someone was trying to wake me.

"They're coming! Please wake up—they're coming over the bridge! Please come quickly!"

I struggled back to consciousness, unable to understand the meaning of these frantic whispers. Who was coming? And why did that mean I had to get up? And what was that other sound in the background—that rhythmic, clanking noise? Fumbling around under my makeshift pillow, I located the rubber-cased torch that I'd put there before snuggling down in my sleeping bag for the night. I switched it on and directed the beam towards the face that was poking through the tent flap. It was the younger of the two boys from the little tent by the bridge, his features contracted with urgency as he blinked in the torchlight.

"They're coming!" he repeated. "You said you'd help us if they came back. They're here—they're coming over the bridge now!"

It all fell into place with a sickening thud. Seven or eight blokes, armed with axes and iron bars, coming back to attack those two lads while they slept. And I had said I'd handle "anything that cropped up." The clanking noise must be the gang approaching via the bridge. They were nearly here, and I was expected to go out into the cold darkness to confront them, armed only with a torch. I must have been mad! Why on earth had I played the hero like that earlier on? I should have told them I was a coward and that their best bet was to pack up and go after all. I would cheerfully have given a million pounds at that moment to have been able to burrow back down into the wonderful warm security of my sleeping bag and forget the whole thing.

"Steve reckons there's about fifteen of 'em this time," came the next panic-stricken whisper, "and they've all got iron bars. I'll go and wait for you by the tent with Steve!"

I knew I had to go, and I knew that the longer I lay there hoping that the nightmare would go away, the more petrified I would become. Sitting up, I worked my sleeping bag down over my hips and drew my knees up to free my feet. I was wearing a thick pullover and underpants. If I was going to be hacked to death I was damned if I was going to submit to it with no trousers on. I leaned forward and found my jeans in the pile of clothing at the end of the tent. If I'd stayed in a sitting position I wouldn't have got into such a tangle. As it was, I was trying to get up and leave the tent at the same time as putting my jeans on. Attempts to shake Mike into waking up had failed completely, fierce whispers were equally useless. The boy's voice sounded again from just outside the tent.

"Please—they've almost reached this end of the bridge! You've got to come!"

I fell backwards out of the tent into the raw night air, one leg in my jeans, the other out. Scrambling awkwardly to my feet, I looked over in the direction of the bridge. Sure enough, a long line of figures showed up sharply against the night sky as they moved towards the wooden steps that gave access to our side of the river. Several of the shadowy forms were holding long straight objects that might easily be iron bars. There was something very macabre about the steady rhythmic clang of their feet on the bridge—it was the sound of an army marching inexorably to the attack.

I was still deeply concerned about the need to be appropriately dressed for the imminent conflict. With my torch clamped under one armpit, I hopped and stumbled over the clammy turf towards the bottom of the steps, trying in vain to get my other leg into the jeans as I went. Ten yards from my objective I knew that my balance had finally gone. My unclothed limb had met an unexpected and quite inexplicable blockage halfway down the left leg of my jeans. My hopping increased to a ludicrous rate as I frantically tried to regain balance. I just caught a glimpse of the two boys' faces as I flew past them on one leg. There were expressions of wonder on their faces. Presumably they thought my strange behaviour was a ploy of some sort, designed to confuse the enemy perhaps. I finally crashed to the ground at the foot of the steps, hitting the earth with a jarring thump. When I looked up, all I could see was the blinding light of a torch shining down onto my face, and I knew that the leader of the attacking force was upon me. I gasped out some words from a throat constricted by fear.

"What you are planning is—is a criminal and immoral act," I croaked, "punishable by imprisonment!"

"Well, you do surprise me," said a pleasantly cultured voice from behind the torch. "I had always understood that night hikes were well within the bounds of law."

The torch was lowered. I picked up my own torch from where it had fallen in the wet grass and, sitting up, shone it towards the speaker. Pleasant, middle-aged face, greying hair, something round his neck—something white. It was a dog collar. I shone my torch around the growing circle of figures who had descended the steps. They were all wearing dog collars. Some carried walking sticks. I was surrounded by vicars. . .

"But you weren't to know, were you, darling? I thought you were very brave. After all, they might have been the other lot, mightn't they?"

It was half an hour later, and Annie and I were sitting in our sleeping bags, beside a temporarily revived camp fire. The 'gang' of vicars, a party from a clergy convention being held at a conference centre on the other side of the valley, had continued their night walk, much amused and stimulated by their unexpected adventure. Mike had finally stumbled out of the tent when the commotion reached its height, and stumbled blearily back again as soon as he gathered that he wasn't needed. I got back from seeing my vicars off, and saying goodnight to two very relieved boys, to find Annie coaxing the embers of the fire back into life with little pieces of wood left over from our collection. She made me sit down and tell her exactly what had happened.

"None of our boys woke up, did they, David?"

"No, they didn't, not so much as a snore from any of them."

I pointed at the tents one by one.

"There's Dennis and Desmond in that one, Anthony and Howard in that one, Colin and Arnold in that one, and Henry and Robert in that one."

"All packed together like little pairs of sardines," said Annie. "Fast asleep without a care in the world."

"That's right," I agreed, staring into the flames, "but only while they're asleep."

We pressed closer together, trying to feel warm enough to stay together a little longer. A minute passed.

"Annie?"

"Mmm?"

"Do you realise what you said just now?"

"What?"

"You said that none of our boys woke up."

"Did I?"

"Yes, you did."

Another minute passed.

"Do you think you will apply for this job, Annie?"

She sighed and leaned her head on my shoulder.

"I rather think I will. I'd feel terribly guilty if I left these kids to put up with you on your own."

"Annie?"

"Yes?"

"You know you said earlier that you were going to kiss me when you got the chance?"

"Yes?"

"Now's your chance. . ."